# Books by Irene Vartanoff

Selkirk Family Ranch Series:
*Captive of the Cattle Baron*
*Saving the Soldier*
*Cowgirl Rescue*
*The Ranch Master*
*Runaway Rancher*
*Becky Lang Rides Again*

Women's Fiction:
*Cleaning Her House*
*A Daughter's a Daughter*
*Summer in the City*

Gothic Romance:
*Second Chance Reunion*

Singers in Love Series:
*Haunted Tenor*
*Friendzoned Soprano*
*Defiant Diva*

Chick Lit Superhero Action Series:
*Temporary Superheroine*
*Crisis at Comicon*

To sign up for my free author newsletter and get your free copy of *Carrie's Story*, a novella in the Selkirk Family Ranch series, visit irenevartanoff.com.

# Captive

## OF THE
## CATTLE BARON

*Irene Vartanoff*

Cover design by BookGraphics.net
Formatting by Polgarus Studio
Copyright © 2015 Irene Vartanoff All rights reserved.

Published by Irene Vartanoff
www.irenevartanoff.com
P.O. Box 27
Gerrardstown, WV 25420


ISBN: 978-0-9861252-2-5
ISBN: 978-0-9861252-3-2 (ebook)

*This book is dedicated to all women*

# Captive
## OF THE
## CATTLE BARON

# Chapter 1

Addie Jelleff tried not to stare at the handsome man standing so near, but she couldn't resist a few discreet peeks. His black Stetson, which he'd touched in gentlemanly acknowledgment when she entered the hotel elevator, proclaimed him a local. Only a confident western man would wear a cowboy hat with an Italian suit.

Tall, muscular, and dark haired, he had chestnut eyes and a strong chin. A manly man. He was the best-looking guy she'd encountered so far in Jackson Hole, Wyoming.

But there was no time for getting acquainted. She must hurry out of the public eye and get safely into Caz's suite before the tabloid reporters cornered her. They had followed her all the way from her ranch to the hotel, where more were camped out. Anything to produce more sensational copy about the shooting. When they'd been distracted by a limo pulling up to the hotel, she'd rushed inside through the hotel garage. Luckily, the hotel wouldn't allow the reporters to stake out the elevators.

Suddenly dizzy, she lurched.

Strong hands helped her remain upright.

"Steady there," came his deep voice.

"Th-thanks," she said, struggling to fight her body's inexplicable weakness. Was it because she'd run so fast a minute ago?

She leaned against the wall, breathing shakily. He remained next to her instead of returning to his side of the elevator.

"I don't know what hit me," she said.

His stare was noncommittal, as if he had an opinion but would not voice it. He still held her shoulders lightly. She was tall for a woman, but he was taller. His touch sent a warm sensation through her, but not enough to conquer the weird feeling that her body was almost weightless. As she tried to remain upright, she anchored her gaze on his face. A multicolored halo surrounded him, as if he was a special being and not just a stranger riding in the same steel box. Although with wood trim that matched the lodge's rustic décor, the elevator didn't look like a steel box. Oh, she was dizzy. Could this be the result of the allergy pill she'd taken?

As she panted, she saw him examine her face. Finally, her breath steadied. Their faces were very close. His chest rose and fell. His lips parted, as if to say or do something. Was he about to kiss her? Would he dare do that to a stranger? Why was she fantasizing about this man when she felt her legs might not keep her upright another minute?

A ding sounded.

"Oh. Here's my floor." She moved to exit, trying and failing to walk normally. Instead of gliding out of the elevator, she nearly stumbled. "I'm okay now."

"You're not," he said. He still had one large hand on her arm.

"I will be," she replied with determination. Reluctantly, she moved away from his protective grasp. Only a few steps and she'd be hidden by a wall and out of sight. She must get to Caz's suite. "Thanks again."

"It was my pleasure." The deep, sonorous voice followed her as she staggered down the corridor.

\*\*\*

Baron Selkirk watched the beautiful blonde weave a meandering path until she turned a corner and drifted out of sight. Only then could he breathe again. The hot blood pounding in his veins finally began to cool off. He allowed the elevator doors to close.

He punched the Door Open button. As the metal walls parted, he lunged between them. He charged down the hotel corridor. Sure enough, once he'd turned the corner, he found her leaning against the wall, half-fainting.

"You're ill," he said. "I'll call the desk for a doctor."

Her eyes widened at his words.

"No, don't," she said. "Don't call anyone."

Was that fear in her expression? What was she afraid of?

"I'm not leaving you alone here to keel over," he said. Although he wasn't touching her, he stood close enough to catch her if she crumpled. Close enough to notice that her blue eyes were very dilated.

She half-lifted one arm and pointed down the hall to

double doors. "Help me to that suite?"

"Lean on me," he said, putting an arm around her soft shoulders. The moment he touched her, a thrill shot through his body. He willed himself to concentrate on getting her to safety.

When they reached the double doors, she disentangled herself and rested against the doorframe. "Thank you. I'll be all right from here."

He frowned. "Where's your key?"

She shook her head. "It's not my suite." She knocked softly on the wood.

Baron spotted a doorbell and reached over to jab it. He kept his finger on the bell until he heard someone approach the door.

"Who is it?" a muffled voice asked.

"It's me," the blonde said.

The person inside must have used the peephole, for his next words were, "I can see you're not alone. Who's he?"

She glanced up at Baron. "A hotel guest. I've been feeling weird. He helped me here."

"Make him leave."

She shrugged. "Thanks for your help," she said to Baron, "but you'd better go now."

He got it. The door wouldn't be opened until he left. "Are you sure you want to do this?" He angled his eyes at the door, indicating his doubts about who and what awaited her inside.

"I'll be okay," she said. "Thank you."

Baron didn't move. This was wrong.

"Please," she said.

He tipped his hat. "Your call. Have a nice life."

Her sudden look of dismay almost made him refuse to budge, but he turned and walked to the elevator, forcing himself to not look back. Once he was a few steps away, he heard the suite door open and muffled words. At the corner, he looked behind him. She was gone.

Back in the elevator, he couldn't stop thinking about her. She'd smelled like flowers. His arms had ached to gather her close. Other parts of his male body had wanted more.

Damn shame. She was ill, or possibly high on something. Like Julie. No, don't go there. Why were all the beautiful women so messed up? Her casual cowgirl duds hadn't hidden a terrific figure, and she'd smiled at him very sweetly. She'd needed help, leaning against the wall, practically fainting. Yet his body had urged him to possess her. Did he have no morals?

He removed his hat and ran his fingers through his hair. His trip to town had been a bust. He'd planned to take a woman friend back with him, but she'd had an emergency at home and had not come to the geology conference after all. Discreet inquiry at the casino had failed to produce anyone who could play the part of his girlfriend credibly. He must have been desperate to even ask, given how much he despised the acting profession.

The beautiful blonde was the only woman he'd seen in Jackson Hole who appealed to him, and no way would he consider getting involved with her—as long as his brain was in charge instead of some other part of his anatomy. Hard to believe he'd found a total stranger so viscerally exciting.

Time was running out. Tess and Paula would arrive at the

ranch in two days for the last surge of the roundup. Tess was messed up lately. Bad enough. But Paula was after him. For marriage, or just an affair? Why she did it was anyone's guess. She was hung up on his brother, JD. His brother. Damn. Try not to think about him. The geology conference was over and the ranch needed its substitute boss.

He replaced the hat, cocking it just right, level with his forehead, not tilted. He should pack up, check out, and start for home after lunch.

The elevator doors opened at the lobby. He'd been so bemused by the gorgeous blonde and her plight, he forgot to get off on his floor.

He punched the elevator button again. This trip to Jackson Hole was a fool's errand. Back in the ranch kitchen, when he announced his plan, he'd thought it was brilliant.

"I'm heading for Jackson Hole. Geology conference. Coming back with a woman friend."

Hoot Hawkins, his elderly, semi-retired ranch manager, had fingered his beard. "Roundup's not over yet, boss."

"You can oversee the next phase. I want someone here to run interference when Tess and Paula arrive."

Hoot frowned. "Your daddy worked with the roundup crew every day."

"I run the ranch my way, not his."

"Sure, boss." Hoot nodded. "But your sister and her friend are plenty distracting at the end of roundup. We don't need no other women."

"Nonsense," replied Miss Betty, turning from the stove to give the older man a quelling glance. "He's a grown man.

Time he found him a woman of his own."

Baron drank his coffee, enjoying the bite of Miss Betty's strong brew. "Tess has a right to come home, no matter what. But Paula has an agenda. She has her eye on me, maybe as her husband. I don't want to spend their whole visit evading her."

"She ain't the type to be happy on a cattle ranch," Hoot said. "You know what that gal told me once? Said the horse I brought her to ride was the wrong color."

Hoot looked as if he wanted to spit in disgust, but didn't dare in Miss Betty's sparkling clean kitchen.

"She was teasing you, you old fool," Miss Betty said.

"More coffee please, Miss Betty," Baron asked. "I need to build up my strength."

She poured him a full cup. "Don't you go bringing back no showgirl from a casino, you hear?"

"Women today are no good." Hoot added. "They're all of them two-faced. 'Cepting you, of course, Miss B."

Miss Betty was not mollified by Hoot's hasty addition of praise for her. She waved a wooden spoon at him. "You been meetin' the wrong kind of gal. So's the boss. Don't go to honky-tonks expectin' to find decent women."

"I don't frequent honky-tonks," Baron replied mildly.

"Hoot does."

"Aw, don't shame me like that, woman. A man can get lonely now and then."

"A man needs a wife, that's what he needs. You should go to church sometime, Hoot. There's good women there."

She turned to him. "You, too, boss. Go find a good woman. That would-be movie star who let you down ain't the only woman in the world."

"Let's not go there."

"Okay, sorry, boss. But she wasn't right for you." She pointed at the TV mounted on a cabinet. It showed an old sitcom. "There's a nice young girl. I'm sure she growed up into a proper young woman."

"Probably became a typical Hollywood drug addict," was his sour comment.

"Now, boss, you got no call to say that. Adrienne Jelleff never got into no trouble. I hear that after the show ended, she even went to college."

Hoot cackled. "If she saved her TV pay, boss, you wouldn't have to worry that she was after your money, neither."

Miss Betty stood up straight, indignant. "I do not mean for the boss to up and go to California and find him an actress. Been there, done that. He should bring home a normal girl who is nice, like the girl on TV."

He set his coffee cup on the table and stood up, taller than both long-time ranch employees. "I'm driving to Jackson Hole. I need to meet up with my colleagues. With luck I'll bring back my woman friend to wave in front of Paula. Spike her efforts to hogtie me."

"Great idea, boss." Hoot encouraged. "Discourage Miss Paula."

Miss Betty was less enthusiastic. "Don't bring back a tourist who thinks this is a dude ranch."

Baron laughed. "If I do, then we'll make Hoot sing cowboy songs by the chuck wagon."

\*\*\*

Addie leaned against the suite door, panting, watching her would-be savior walk away. When that handsome cowboy had loomed so close, she'd wanted to sink into his broad chest and forget everything but the strength of his arms around her. He'd wanted it, too. There had been something in his eyes. Or was she fantasizing his interest was more than a stranger's concern for someone who was ill?

If only this weird faintness would abate, she could get safely into Caz's suite before some sneaky tabloid reporter found her. But waves kept sweeping over her. She felt wretched. It had to be that allergy pill.

"Caz, open up. He's gone."

The other door opened. Caz cast a cautious glance around the deserted hotel corridor then dragged her inside.

"You look terrible," he said.

"I feel dizzy."

"You do look pale. But you're not wearing makeup. And what's with the cowboy shirt and the boots? Where have those boots been? Your stable? You're not on the horse farm now."

As he spoke, he led her through the entrance hall and into a spacious living room with an enormous chalet window.

"It's called a ranch in the west," she replied. Then the panorama of the outdoors stopped her in her tracks.

"Wow. What a great view." His suite windows opened to the snow-capped mountains and wooded valleys and the Snake River below. "This is fantastic." The windows overlooked the ski runs, but also caught the middle of town and the hills going north. Every part of Jackson Hole was visible.

Caz didn't even glance in the direction of the outdoors. He flung himself down on a couch. "I'm sick of being cooped up."

Addie lingered at the window, identifying local landmarks like her favorite western wear store, but mostly enjoying the comprehensive view of the hills and the river. She could even see the road leading to her small forty-acre spread, which was just barely visible if she craned her neck all the way to the far end of the huge vee-shaped chalet windows.

"Did you come to visit me or the scenery?" he asked.

She turned away from the mesmerizing beauty of Wyoming to face a stunning example of human genetic beauty. Caz was a golden god, his blond hair set off by piercing blue eyes, regular features, and a body toned in Hollywood gyms and California surf. Her brother, in all but blood.

"Don't be grumpy," she said. "I've been trapped indoors a lot lately, too, because of the paparazzi." Feeling shaky again, she collapsed into a deep chair opposite the couch. She yawned.

Caz glared at her. "Don't take a nap now. I need your help." He leapt up and paced in agitation. "I sent the handlers away today. I'm sick of being cooped up here."

"Some prison," she muttered. The suite was spacious, with a breakfast bar and a full kitchen, and what looked like a dining or conference room beyond. Plus multiple bedrooms and baths, no doubt, off the foyer where she'd entered. Caz's accommodations were larger than most Los Angeles apartments. The rustic lodge theme of the hotel was carried out in the moose-antler lamps flanking the couches, sitting on yellow pine end tables, and a pine coffee table. The couches and chairs were buttery leather, in browns that toned with the highly varnished wood accents all through the rooms. And there was that amazing view.

Yet it meant nothing to Caz, the ultimate city boy. He'd come to Wyoming to visit her, not check out the scenery or the lodge. Now he was in trouble.

He had the television on. A cable crime talk show host notorious for turning tragedies into tabloid scandals held forth.

Addie gestured toward the TV. "A classic movie would be more soothing."

He picked up the remote and clicked off the television. "They say my case will be the trial of the century."

"Exaggeration to incite the viewers. Anyway, there's no such thing as bad publicity when you're an actor."

"What about Fatty Arbuckle? One wild party ruined his career." His pacing took on additional frenzy and he put his fingers to his temples as if he had a headache.

She rolled her eyes. "That Hollywood scandal happened almost a hundred years ago. The public today doesn't expect you to be a saint."

"Oh, yes, they do. Because I played an adorable little boy on *Golden Days*."

She smirked. "I was equally adorable as your sister. We were the adorable brats of network sitcom viewing."

He didn't laugh as she'd hoped.

"I stayed out of trouble my whole life and now this," he said.

"The dirt they're tossing won't stick."

"If only I didn't have to stay here and wait." His voice rose.

She sighed. "Only a few more days. I'll testify, and the D.A. will drop the charges. Or the jury will exonerate you. Or the judge will dismiss the case. Or something. You've got good lawyers working for you."

He threw himself down on the end of the longest couch. "My life will never be the same again," he moaned.

"What about mine?" she retorted. "I was living in happy obscurity until your stalker ex caused this media frenzy by shooting himself in my house."

"Leslie wasn't my ex. It was just a hookup," he insisted.

"Someone obviously didn't get the message," she said. "And now my nice quiet life as a horse whisperer is in shambles."

"I don't understand why you ditched acting to clean up after horses."

"Horses are very intelligent and empathetic creatures. Unlike most directors and producers," she said with a smile.

He finally laughed a little, as she'd meant him to. "Got that right."

"I like horses. I stopped liking acting."

"But why Wyoming, when you could have stayed in California?"

"Haven't we had this conversation before?" She burrowed deeper into the soft leather chair. Her head still felt funny. The dizziness came and went. Amazing what one prescription allergy pill could do.

"In L.A., nobody would have made a big deal out of what happened," Caz said as he tugged nervously on his shirt sleeves, aligning them just so.

She snorted. "You'd be news anywhere because your career is red hot."

"Once the public is convinced I'm a heartless seducer, my career will tank."

"Caz, that's not going to happen. The local D.A. wants to make a name for himself, but there is no case. Leslie pulled a gun and shot himself. End of story."

He rubbed the back of his neck. "Yeah, you're right. Why am I so worried? People stalk actors all the time."

Dragging herself upright, she stood. She moved over to the couch, still feeling wobbly, and sat next to him. Putting one arm across his shoulders, she said, "Because you're a good person, you feel guilty about Leslie's unhinged behavior. But none of this is your fault."

"I've told myself that over and over. Relationships start with hookups," he replied, jumping up. "You meet someone, you have sex, and then maybe you might begin a relationship."

She made a moue of distaste. "Twenty-first century romance. Another reason I moved out to where people take life slower."

"Don't the local dudes try?" he stopped pacing to ask.

"They take no for an answer when I'm riding my stallion," she said.

"If only Leslie hadn't followed me here," he fretted.

***

After two hours of trying to calm Caz down or distract him with little success, Addie left his suite. He'd finally taken his anti-anxiety medicine. When they'd worked together as kids on the TV show, Caz was always anxious. He wanted to be perfect. He was still hypersensitive to criticism despite his grown-up success in a hit television action series.

She couldn't eliminate Caz's anxiety, but at least her testimony would end this nightmare. No crime had been committed, after all. Unless shooting yourself was a crime in Wyoming. Maybe it was. If so, Leslie Tone probably would have a choice of jail time or mental health treatment.

She cautiously checked the corridor. No tabloid reporters were in sight, but she didn't want to risk the elevator again and walk out into a lobby full of paparazzi. She headed for the exit stairs.

In the stair shaft, she got that shaky feeling again. She grasped the banister tightly as she struggled down the several flights. The lunch Caz ordered had made her feel better, but now the dizziness had returned.

The hotel didn't have many floors, but the trip down the steps seemed to drag on. Unlike the paneled hotel corridors, the stairs were utilitarian concrete and steel surrounded by painted cinderblock walls. They offered no comfort. She was lightheaded and exhausted. Not a good combo for driving back to the ranch. She should find a place to rest. She should return to Caz's suite and ask to use his second bedroom for a nap. No, if tabloid reporters were watching, that wouldn't look good. She was Caz's friend. There had never been anything else between them.

Besides, she didn't feel strong enough to retrace her steps back up to his suite. Maybe she could rest unnoticed in her vehicle.

The ground floor exit door left her in a service corridor. It also lacked the fancy wooden paneling and sconces made of fake antlers that decorated the public areas of the hotel. The walls were painted a simple white, and the floor was linoleum. At one end, a steel door had a small window that looked like a two-way mirror. It offered a comprehensive view of the lobby.

She peeked through it, and her heart sank. The reception area teemed with reporters, reporters who had recognized her from her TV fame a decade ago despite her low-key western clothing and lack of makeup.

She turned in the other direction. Even walking to the second door was an effort. It opened to the hotel garage, which was on ground level. She went through the door, closing it quietly after her, and began searching for her car.

A shout came from the garage's entrance. "There's Adrienne Jelleff!"

She ducked, then dodged behind a concrete post and kept moving. Feeling dizzier than ever, she paused to catch her breath behind a large black SUV. Running footsteps and shouts echoed off the concrete. The reporters could be coming from any direction. Desperately, she tore at the SUV's back door handle. It opened, and she tumbled in. She pulled a blanket over herself and hid.

The footsteps and the shouting voices came nearer. Her heart beat fast. Someone opened the driver's door. She was cornered.

"No, sir, I didn't see anyone."

Indistinct words. Then the reply. "I'd like to help, but a guest is waiting for this vehicle."

A hotel employee, then.

He hopped in and started the engine. Only a few seconds later, he stopped the vehicle.

A new voice spoke. "The owner's getting some coffee for the road, Jake. Park it on the side for now." In a few seconds, the driver had parked and exited the SUV, slamming the door.

Was she safe to leave now? The SUV was probably at the hotel's main entrance. She'd have nowhere to hide if she climbed out immediately. Perhaps if she waited a minute or two, the reporters would stop acting like a pack of deranged hounds. She had a little time before the car owner came out.

Her head hurt. She was very tired. She closed her eyes.

***

Baron drove the deserted hill road and considered his situation. The trip hadn't panned out. Because of the ranch, he'd had to pass up opportunities for new geology assignments. He'd had no luck finding someone to run interference for him with Paula. The only memorable moment of his visit to Jackson had been the blonde in the elevator. Too bad about her.

Usually the long drive was restorative. Outside the town, which often was overrun by tourists, the peaceful and mostly empty Wyoming countryside was a pleasure to behold. Hills gave way to less rugged territory, and the dark green fir trees to shorter, paler scrub as he drove south. He seldom encountered more than a few other vehicles on the road, and there never was the kind of traffic he experienced on Jackson's few but congested streets.

Today his thoughts weren't calmed by the scenery, as they dwelled on the situation awaiting him. He had the sole responsibility for running the family's vast ranch, including roundup. What was to have been a temporary fill-in had dragged on for a year, with no end in sight. He ought to suck it up and keep on doing his duty, but he was restive. The ranch hands didn't like to obey his orders, yet his father didn't do anything to help long distance. To keep peace in his family, Baron also had to allow his sister's frequent visits, and along with her, Paula. Tess had been in bad shape lately, drinking way too much. Paula acted like her keeper, and he supposed he should feel grateful since Tess wouldn't listen to him. But then Paula turned around and chased him. He wasn't interested, and he doubted she really was. Paula often disparaged the ranch, saying it was too remote from civilization.

Although how remote was a place with its own airplane and landing strip? Not very. When he needed to go somewhere in a hurry, he had no problem. But he liked the drive to Jackson Hole. It had some of the most beautiful natural scenery in the world.

Beautiful scenery reminded him again of that woman. Damn. He shouldn't have left her at that suite door. Nothing good had waited for her inside, he was convinced. A drug dealer, maybe? She'd been so helpless, but determined. He should have stepped up and saved her.

The highway was deserted the whole way. Usually, he

played music, but today he wasn't in the mood. A small *thunk* came from the back of the vehicle. He checked the rearview mirror. Nothing unusual that he could see.

There. There was a sound again. A scraping noise. Was it coming from the luggage area?

He pulled the SUV to the side of the road and shut the engine. Could an animal have somehow gotten in while the SUV was garaged? He'd hardly looked in the vehicle when he tossed his case into the back seat.

He unlocked the glove compartment and retrieved his pistol. After slowly stepping down to the pavement, he walked around to the back of his SUV. In one smooth movement, he opened the gate and pointed his gun.

Wrapped in his emergency blanket, the beautiful woman from the hotel stared up at him.

# Chapter 2

"Would you consider lowering your piece?" Addie asked the man towering over her, holding what was no doubt a loaded gun. This was the west. Men didn't point unless they were prepared to shoot. "I'm unarmed," she said, very slowly pulling her hands from beneath the blanket, trying not to freak out at the danger she was in.

He dropped the arm holding the pistol.

"What the hell are you doing in my SUV?"

She took a breath then held it as he stared at her. Where to start? "Uh, it's complicated. I fell asleep."

"Drugs?"

"What?"

"You were loopy," he said, frowning. "In the hotel. Your eyes were dilated. Still are. What drug are you strung out on?"

She shook her head. "No. You don't understand."

"Don't deny the truth." He stashed his pistol in his belt behind his back. He leaned in and pulled her out. She stumbled trying to get her balance. The dizziness was still there.

"You're still riding the high, whatever it is," he said.

He took her stumble as proof she was under the influence of illegal drugs. She wanted to argue, but the threat of fainting was too near.

"You'd better sit up front." He marched her to the passenger side of his vehicle. After he opened the door, he lifted her toward the seat, acting as if her weight was nothing. He paused with her in his arms. Their glances connected. Was that anger in his expression, or something else? She shivered. Did he intend to kiss her? Why did she keep thinking that? Did she want him to kiss her? She was in big trouble here, but her body was sending signals as though she was on a date with a lover.

He set her down on the seat, backed away, and stared at her. He shook it off and firmly snapped the seat harness over her.

"Stay put," he commanded, and slammed her door.

When had a man picked her up like that? Never. When had a man she was attracted to looked at her as if he wanted to devour her? Never.

She shivered again. She felt so weak. She rested her head limply on the headrest. Behind her came the noise of him throwing the blanket inside and shutting the back gate. He moved around to the driver's seat and got in, depositing his gun in the side pocket of his door.

When he turned on the motor, she roused herself to ask, "Where are you taking me?"

\*\*\*

*Anywhere you'll let me,* was his thought, but he didn't answer aloud. She was still loaded with whatever she'd done to harm herself. Or someone had given her a second dose? The man in the hotel suite? It had been a man, Baron was sure. Once he had her safely at his ranch, he'd see to it that she cleaned up. He could save her.

"Where are we going?" she asked again, more urgency in her voice.

"I'm heading home."

"Where's that?"

"My spread is about two hundred miles south of Jackson Hole."

"Wait. How do I get back?"

He looked over at her briefly, seeing the worry on her face. Fear for her safety with him, or about losing contact with her dealer?

"I need to go back," she repeated.

"This isn't a bus service," he replied. "I'm nearly home. You chose to come along for the ride."

"No." She shook her head. "No, I didn't. I ran away—" She caught herself. "I mean, I was dizzy. I had to rest. I didn't intend to stow away and take a trip."

"Maybe you didn't." He shrugged. "But we're more than halfway there already. I'm not turning back at this point."

"Why not?" Exasperation tinged her voice. "We don't know each other. You can drop me in the nearest town, and I'll figure it out."

"There aren't any towns between here and my place. I'm not letting you off just anywhere to wander around in a drug-induced stupor."

"You have the wrong idea about me. I took an allergy pill. That's all."

Maybe she was telling the truth, or maybe she'd made more than one wrong choice in her life to be in such a condition. He didn't want to let her sink into self-destruction. The calm of his ranch and the help of his housekeeper would straighten up this beauty.

"What's your name?" he asked.

She pouted.

"Tell me your name. Don't be stubborn." He took his eyes off the winding road for a second to look at her again. She had her arms folded across her chest.

"Addie," she said.

"Just Addie? What about a last name?"

"Addie Smith," she said, her intonation making it clear that was not her real last name.

"Pleased to make your acquaintance, Ms. Smith."

She replied. "I'm not happy to make yours, under the circumstances. And anyway, don't you have a name?"

"Baron Selkirk."

She stared at him. "You're a baron? You have a title?"

"My mother has a sense of humor. She decided a cattle baron should be named Baron."

She smothered a laugh. "Okay, you're as American as I am. Then you have no excuse for not honoring my civil rights."

He glanced over at her again. She looked so cute when she thought she'd won an argument. He wouldn't let her fall back into the clutches of whoever did this to her.

"This is a one-way drive," he said. "My housekeeper will take charge of you. You'll return to your home, I promise."

"I should be reassured, I suppose." There was sarcasm in her voice. "If I can believe you."

He stopped the SUV in the middle of the road, and turned in her direction. She sat up stiffly, as if steeling herself against a blow.

"Addie Smith, or Jones, or whatever, you have my solemn word that you are in no physical danger from me." He searched her face for any hint that she believed him. What he saw was caution. Smart woman.

"I won't leave you here in the middle of nowhere, defenseless," he said. "Once we're at the ranch, and you've had a chance to detox, then we'll talk about getting you back to Jackson Hole."

Before he could start the engine, she was clawing at the door. The handle didn't budge.

"Custom child lock system for my dog," he explained, as she continued to wrestle with it. She cast him a fraught glance.

"You're safe with me," he repeated. "But I won't let you hurt yourself."

Her voice came out strangled. "This is wrongful imprisonment. It's a crime."

"I want to help you get sober."

"You have a hell of a nerve judging me. You don't know anything about me."

He wanted to know everything there was to know about Addie so-not-Smith. He could turn the vehicle around and take her back to Jackson Hole. The drive wasn't that long. But he didn't want to. He'd found her and he wanted to keep her.

***

Frustrated, Addie stared at her gallant captor, the man determined to save her from herself. He paid attention to the road, although the ribbon of highway hardly merited attention. Endless desert. Not a single road crossing theirs. She'd never been to this southern part of Wyoming. It looked empty. Sand or some kind of light-colored dirt supported scraggly bushes and shorter grasses and weeds. No trees. She saw no houses. Not even abandoned industrial buildings. There were no paved roads crossing the highway. No dirt tracks leading off it to hidden ranches. Nothing.

Despite her attempt to bail and her big words, she didn't want him to dump her at the nearest gas station in the middle of nowhere. She had a wallet in her pocket, but a credit card and forty dollars wouldn't necessarily get her back home with ease.

A wave of faintness washed over her. She leaned her head back, unable to keep it upright. Finally, the dizziness passed, but every inch of her body felt weirdly weak. How could she hurl herself at him and wrestle him for control of the SUV when every other minute she was on the edge of collapse?

He was clean cut. He spoke well. He obviously was the take-charge type. He kept mentioning his housekeeper, as if he was taking Addie to a civilized, respectable home. He'd helped her at the hotel, so maybe she could trust him. Not that she could leap out of the SUV, anyway. Her door wouldn't open. She supposed she could lower the window and try to crawl out. If she could move, which felt impossible.

24

If she succeeded, she might kill herself falling onto the highway. More likely he'd stop the vehicle and haul her butt inside. There'd be an undignified physical struggle. She'd been in his strong arms twice already. Each time, she'd felt a physical thrill despite how sick she was. If they started wrestling over her trying to escape, he might lose control. The idea was far too enticing. If she'd felt better, she might have risked it. He was hot. Too bad she felt so lousy.

Her mind was wandering, too. Who thinks about a stranger's hotness when he might be a serial killer? Or an opportunistic rapist, not the decent sort he presented as? A decent but high-handed and annoying control freak. What could she do? She was already his captive. She'd fight him, of course.

She was so dizzy. Rest for now. Be ready to fight if the need arose. She was in a terrible jam, but if she stayed cool, she'd find her opportunity. She hoped.

First, she must recover. She'd never, ever take an allergy medicine again. She'd bear with sneezing and congestion and runny eyes from now on.

\*\*\*

Baron spared a glance from the road and saw his stowaway was asleep again. She was under the influence of a very strong drug. He was doing the right thing taking her to where she could be cared for. Miss Betty was a motherly type and she was a trained nurse. She would look after Addie Smith.

He turned his gaze back to the highway. He'd lied a little to his unwilling guest. He could take a crossing road in a few miles that would lead to a town eventually, although it had almost nothing, just a gas station and a couple of stores. Once they were at his ranch, he could easily fly her back to Jackson Hole if she needed serious medical attention. He was doing the right thing.

Miss Betty had urged him to find a new girlfriend who was nice. Instead, he was bringing back a feisty dish who had a drug problem. But there was something about her…

\*\*\*

Addie opened her eyes when the SUV jolted.

"Just the cattle guard. We're on the ranch road," his voice came from next to her.

She sat up and stretched a little. "Oh, my. I thought I'd dreamed this craziness."

"Nope. You're in the real world."

She cocked her head at him. "You're enjoying this, aren't you? Do you make a habit of abducting strange women?"

A sneaky grin played around his mouth, but his answer was deadpan. "Do it all the time."

"I hope not. A felony conviction would lose you your right to vote or to carry that Smith & Wesson."

He glanced at the weapon in the door pocket. "I keep it in the car in case of vermin. More discreet than racking a shotgun when I'm not on my own property."

He pointed ahead. "The ranch house will come into sight in a minute, over this rise."

Where he'd indicated, the land took a small dip, and then rose. Mostly the land was flat, but white-capped mountains were pale lavender at the horizon. This ranch was a long way from anywhere.

Her so-called host had an odd sense of distance. It was at least a mile before they went up the rise, and another mile beyond that when the ranch house came into view. Baron Selkirk had a large spread, much, much bigger than hers. Maybe that's why he was a baron. A highhanded man used to being in charge.

It was a real ranch. Thank god. A well-kept and large ranch house dominated a group of buildings that included a barn and outbuildings. Maybe he wasn't a serial killer after all. He might still be a creep, though he seemed like a decent enough guy—although a domineering and stubborn type. Instead of fighting for her life, she could concentrate on fighting for her personal freedom. She couldn't let some strange man, hot as he was, abduct her.

She must call her ranch manager and tell him where she was, or he'd soon be contacting the state police to initiate a search.

Baron pulled the SUV in front of the main house and honked the horn. He got out and came around the SUV to let Addie out. She'd already taken off her seatbelt, but he stopped her attempt to hop down. He lifted her bodily out of the seat, and held her in his arms.

Pleasurable sensations washed over her. His arms were so strong. His chest was large and hard, yet somehow comfortable. Her body automatically relaxed against his, as if she was meant to be held so closely by this man.

"Put me down. I can walk," she said, fighting the urge to nestle.

"What's the matter, boss?" A middle-aged woman wearing an apron called anxiously from the large front porch. "Who's that?"

"Put me down," Addie repeated, louder.

"Put your arms around me and enjoy the free ride," he replied. He turned to the housekeeper with Addie firmly in his embrace. "Got a visitor, Miss Betty." He carried Addie up the steps with no visible effort. His breathing didn't even change.

Addie's did. What man had ever carried her like this? Effortlessly, confidently, as if she belonged in his arms? She had to get hold of herself. Baron's manly display of strength could not be allowed to turn her into mush, although she was afraid that's exactly what had happened. She tingled all over with feminine delight.

"Is she sick?" Miss Betty asked.

"No," Baron replied.

"Yes," Addie said.

Miss Betty put her hands on her hips and said, "Well, you two better make up your minds."

"I'll put her in the blue guest room. That okay with you?"

"Sure, boss."

"What if it's not okay with me?" Addie asked.

Miss Betty opened the screen door. "Come on inside. No need to wrangle where the cattle can hear y'all."

Baron carried Addie through the porch and into a large entrance hall. He headed for the staircase.

28

"I can walk," Addie said. "Let me down."

"Considering the trouble you have walking, why risk falling down the stairs?"

"I won't fall. I'm all right now."

"Let's not test that out."

As they argued, he carried her up the steps, again without showing any visible strain. Addie had never met a man so determined to treat her like a fragile flower. That and the warmth of his body holding hers were insidiously appealing. She must resist. They finally reached a large guest bedroom with blue paint on the walls.

Baron set her down on the queen-sized bed, settling her head on the pillow. "Lie down," he ordered.

Addie sat up immediately. As she did, the dizziness returned. "Ohhh." She put her hand to her forehead.

"You're still under the influence. You need to rest and get it out of your system." He turned to Miss Betty, who had followed them and was now standing by the door. "Would you check her out?"

"What's wrong with her, boss?"

"Drugs."

"No, that's not true," Addie protested. She tried to remain upright, to prove she was all right, but her head was spinning.

"Looks like you're feelin' dizzy," Miss Betty said.

"I don't know what drug she took, but she could hardly stand up when I first encountered her. She slept in the SUV for hours," Baron told the housekeeper.

Miss Betty advanced to the bed and laid the surprisingly soft back of her hand on Addie's forehead. "No fever. How do you feel, miss?"

Addie roused herself enough to glare at Baron. "I'll answer, but not with this—this kidnapper listening."

Miss Betty turned to Baron. "Shoo. We're gonna talk women talk. You go wrestle cattle, or somethin'."

To Addie's surprise, Baron yielded with a good grace. "Yes, ma'am. You take good care of her." He shot a meaningful glance at Addie. "Rest and recover."

After he'd closed the bedroom door behind him, Miss Betty turned back to Addie.

"I'm Betty Strauss."

"Addie. Addie Smith. Or Jones. Or whatever."

Miss Betty nodded. "Got it. What's wrong with you?"

"I'm woozy. It comes and goes," Addie said.

"I was a nurse's aide ten years. Come clean with me. You on drugs?"

"I took just one pill, a prescription twenty-four hour allergy medicine, after my regular sinus pill didn't work," Addie said. She named the medication. "Big mistake."

Miss Betty asked her more questions, then took her pulse. "Normal," she said. She also grabbed a thermometer from the bathroom medicine cabinet and took Addie's temperature. "Normal." The older women clicked her tongue in disapproval. "When you first felt bad, you should have called your doctor or the pharmacy."

"I didn't think about that." Addie leaned back on the pillow. "I'm sleepy and dizzy."

Miss Betty went to the bureau and opened a drawer. She pulled out a nightgown. "Let me help you to the bathroom.

Then you should do as the boss says and rest."

"I can walk. I don't need help." Addie stood up unaided. She wavered as the dizziness returned. "Oh."

Miss Betty put a strong arm around her. "Now, don't fall on me, child, or we'll have to call Baron to get you to the bathroom."

"Is he always so take charge?"

"It's been growin'. Lean on me."

With slow and careful motions, they got Addie to the bathroom, where she freshened up and changed into the nightgown. Then it was back to the bed with Miss Betty's aid. The older woman had turned down the covers for her.

Addie lay under a thin blue quilt, worn out from walking only a few feet. She watched Miss Betty draw the shades and collect the clothes from the bathroom.

"I'll wash your things, but we got plenty extras you can use. They're in the bureau and that closet." The older woman indicated a door Addie hadn't noticed previously.

"Thank you." Addie hesitated, but it had to be said. "Please check on me from time to time. I should have gone to the emergency room when this started happening."

"You feelin' worse than before?" The old lady's face showed concern.

"No, but the dizziness scares me. So does being stuck in the middle of nowhere," Addie said, exhaustion in her voice and in every pore of her body.

"Now, don't you worry. This ranch is isolated, but we can fly you to a hospital in jig time."

Addie shuddered. "I hope it won't come to that."

"Sleep now. I'll check on you," Miss Betty said as she left the bedroom door slightly ajar.

Addie knew she should be more upset about Baron's highhanded behavior, but she felt so tired. She slept.

\*\*\*

Miss Betty cornered Baron in the kitchen, where he was helping himself to peanut butter and jelly. She slapped his fingers.

"'Tain't enough to hold you. I'll make you a sandwich."

She busied herself pulling out meat and fixings. "Did you really abduct that girl?"

He leaned back in the kitchen chair. He let out a long breath. "Not exactly. Maybe."

"Which is it?" came the sharp retort.

He took a napkin from the stack of checkered cloths in the center of the table. Then he poured himself lemonade from the pitcher he'd pulled from the refrigerator.

"Well?"

"She'd stowed away in the back of the SUV. I didn't know she was there. She woke up when I was only a half-hour from here."

"Bein' a decent man, you didn't leave her there in the middle of nowhere," Miss Betty said.

"It wasn't as if she could wait on the next corner for a bus."

Miss Betty snorted. "No buses anywhere." She presented him with a large sandwich on homemade whole-wheat bread. "Why didn't you turn around and take her back to Jackson Hole?"

"She needs protection," he replied.

"From what?"

"From herself, most likely. Maybe from some man."

Miss Betty took a glass from a cabinet and sat down opposite him at the table. She poured herself lemonade. "You're actin' like she's your relative and you have a responsibility to look after her."

"Guess I am. It comes natural to me."

"Don't think so." She snorted. "You took one look at her and thought 'mine.'"

"She looked lost." Baron frowned at the sandwich. "She's taken some drug and maybe she'll sleep it off. If she's seriously ill, I'm ready to fly her to a hospital."

"Her pulse was normal. No fever. She's breathin' okay, but I'll check on her. It don't pay to take chances. Do you know her real name?"

"No."

"She had a wallet in her pants pocket, but she took it to bed with her. I wouldn't feel right sneakin' a peek unless she got a lot sicker," Miss Betty said.

"There might be somebody worried about her by now."

Miss Betty said, "Lots of young women live alone. Maybe not."

Baron squelched a selfish wish that Addie did indeed live all by herself. "She doesn't wear a wedding ring," he said.

Miss Betty shot him a dark look. "You checked, did you? Don't you take any liberties."

"No, ma'am," he said.

Miss Betty's voice was stern. "I mean it. You've practically kidnapped this girl, even if she is ill. Don't you go abusin' the situation."

He said, "I'm not that kind of man. Although I admit Addie brings out a strong protective streak in me."

"Protective streak? That's what they call it these days?" She cackled, then rose and took his empty plate to the sink. "Now go about your business. I'll take good care of the girl."

Baron unwillingly stood up and grabbed his hat. He cast a longing look in the direction of the guest room.

"Shoo, boy. Get outta my kitchen."

# Chapter 3

Addie woke in the night, finally alert. She remembered Miss Betty taking her temperature and pulse a few times. The housekeeper had left a thermos of cool water, but Addie was hungry. During one of her visits, Miss Betty turned the light on in the bathroom, so Addie wasn't lost in the dark.

She stretched and then tested her strength by getting up and heading for the bathroom. No dizziness.

Back in the bedroom, she turned on a light, and sat cross-legged on the bedcovers to take stock of her situation. She was nominally a captive of a rancher named Baron Selkirk, whose spread was large enough to encompass miles just along the entry drive. His housekeeper exuded respectability. Of course, he could be a kinky rich man whose wealth allowed him to get away with murder, but Addie didn't think so.

Getting back to Jackson Hole might be difficult. Baron thought she was some kind of drug addict. What a joke. The pill she took hit her so hard because she didn't take prescription medicines and had no resistance built up. Never again.

For now, she was stuck. If she understood the direction they'd gone, they were somewhere in the southwestern part of Wyoming. She didn't know the state's geography well. She'd only lived in Wyoming for two years. It wasn't as big a state as California, but it was sparsely populated. She'd need Baron's cooperation to get back to Jackson Hole.

Caz's trial started in two days. According to his lawyer, her testimony would likely be needed on the third day, once a jury had been selected. Even getting together a jury took time. So she had at most a week, counting the weekend, to get back home.

She was hungry, and it was probably the middle of the night. She should call her ranch manager, Trudy, and tell him what happened.

This guest bedroom did not have a clock. She had her wallet, but where was her cell phone? In Baron's SUV?

She vaguely remembered Miss Betty promising to wash her clothes. Not that the jeans needed washing, but she had not been in a fit state earlier today—or was it already yesterday?—to protest. A robe was spread on a chair. She put it on and softly opened her bedroom door, ready to investigate her temporary abode.

A few dim lights were on downstairs, possibly for her sake. She found her way to the kitchen. A large wall clock showed it was past two a.m.

A wrapped plate of cookies sat on the kitchen counter. She brought the plate to the table, and opened the refrigerator. A large pitcher held iced tea. Perfect.

She was seated at the kitchen table, munching cookies,

when Baron ambled in.

"Are you feeling better?"

He was in sweatpants and a loose white t-shirt, but barefoot. His hair was tousled, as if he'd been in bed.

"Sorry I woke you. I was hungry," she said.

"Miss Betty told me she was leaving you some cookies."

"Why do you call her Miss Betty?"

He shrugged. "It's an old-fashioned southern form of respectful address. Seems to fit."

"Is she your only employee?"

"In the house? Yes. I've got a ranch manager. We have a couple dozen full-timers, and during roundup we have extra workers. They live over the next hill, in their own compound."

"So they'll be trooping in here at dawn to be fed?"

He shook his head. "No, we've got a separate mess hall and a cook. He lives with the ranch hands."

"This is a big operation, then."

He nodded. "What I've described is only part of it."

"How do I get home?"

"First, you have to be ready."

"I'm fine now. That sinus medicine I took knocked me for a loop, but the weird side effects have worn off."

He shook his head, clearly disbelieving. "Sinus medicine. That's a funny name for an illegal drug that made you loopy."

She frowned. "My doctor gave me a prescription medication. Maybe it combined with the over-the-counter pill I took a few hours before."

She spared a thought about how the tabloids would have turned her sudden illness into a four-page spread about her "struggle with addiction" if she'd collapsed in the hotel. Baron had saved her from that, but he still had the wrong idea about her.

"Aren't you acting a little over-concerned?" she asked. "We shared an elevator, and then you helped me down the hall. Hitching a ride in your SUV was accidental."

"Why did you get inside and hide under the blanket? It's not the most comfortable place to sleep it off."

"I wasn't looking to sleep it off, as you call it." Thoughts about what lies to tell him, or maybe the truth, coursed through her brain. She didn't want to get him involved in her mess. Or see his attitude toward her change because of who the tabloids painted her to be. "I...uh...I was trying to avoid somebody. An old boyfriend," she added, in a burst of inspiration.

"From your accent, you sound like a newcomer to the state. How would you have an old boyfriend who just happens to be at the same luxury hotel?"

"That's the problem with old boyfriends," she replied, daring him to disbelieve her. "They pop up in the darnedest places."

"Right." He shifted in his chair. "Why were you at the hotel?"

"I don't have to tell you."

"I'm not a cop. Why not tell me?"

"It's not your business, that's why." No reason to spill about the scandal. Better give him something. "Actually, I was...I was interviewing for a position."

"What kind of position?" From his expression, he didn't

think it was something respectable.

"Not what you're thinking," she said. "What gives you the right to pass judgment on me?"

When he said nothing, she threw him a bone. "As a horse trainer."

Baron looked skeptical.

"With a visitor from out of town," she added.

His lack of response indicated he didn't believe her.

She sent him an exasperated look. "Forget why I was there. When can you arrange transportation for me back to Jackson Hole?"

"Do you have a job?"

"Of course I have a job," she cried.

"Give me your boss's phone number. I'll inform him that you're taking some time off."

"You're not in charge of my life."

"Don't be stubborn."

"I am not being stubborn. And don't try that typical male thing of criticizing my behavior instead of sticking to the point," she said.

He blinked. "Strong words from a woman who was more than half-addled all day from drugs."

She stood. He stood, too. Somebody had taught him old-fashioned manners. Maybe that was the problem. He was old-fashioned domineering, too.

"I'm not staying here. I'm going back to Jackson," she said.

"That's an old song title," he said with a half-smile. "Nancy Sinatra and Lee Hazelwood. They meant Mississippi."

She gave a woof of frustration. "Hello. We're not playing a

nostalgia game. We're talking about me. My life."

He leaned against the counter and watched her pace. "Why don't you go on back to bed? You're wearing yourself out again."

"I'm not some frail invalid who can't handle a little walking."

"After seeing you almost pass out several times, I'd dispute that."

She took a deep breath. "I'm grateful for your help when I was sick. I'm not sick anymore. I want to go home."

"Is Jackson Hole your home?"

"What difference does it make? That's where my Jeep is, so, yes, I want to return to Jackson Hole." She searched his face for any sign that he was moved by her arguments. Seeing none, she took another exasperated turn around the room. "You have no right to rule my life in any way."

"We'll talk about this after you've fully recovered. Right now you're just tiring yourself out." His pronouncement was completely calm. His deep voice held no mirror of the emotional turmoil she felt.

"Why do I get the feeling that you do not want to cooperate and arrange to get me back north?" she cried.

"Because it's true."

Her mouth dropped open.

"You were in sad shape earlier today," he said. "Would it hurt you to stay here for a while and recover fully?"

"If it was my free choice, that would be different," she said, crossing her arms and glaring at him.

"At this moment, I don't believe you're in any shape to

make a rational free choice about yourself, so I'm choosing for you. For now, you stay on my ranch, where you will be safe and can recover." His expression was adamant.

She stared at him. "You lay down the law and expect me to accept it? No way."

His demeanor didn't change.

She let out an exasperated breath. "We're getting nowhere."

"Then go back to bed. Rest."

She glared at him. Behind him, the wall clock said 2:30 a.m. Even if he suddenly changed his mind and agreed to take her home, it couldn't happen in the middle of the night. "I've had enough of this," she said.

He'd defeated her for the moment, but only for the moment, she promised herself. She walked toward the kitchen door. "Good night."

He moved away from the stove to intercept her. "No need to wear yourself out all over again. I'll carry you up," he said.

She stopped dead. Being in his arms, alone with him, in the middle of the night? That would be asking for trouble. "No, thanks. I'm good."

"Are you?" Baron gave her whole body a comprehensive look, but lingered on her face. His eyes held an expression she understood all too well. What he wanted from her in the middle of the night was clear.

Her breath was giving her trouble again. Her limbs tingled and her breasts ached. She whirled and sped out of the kitchen, not daring to look back. It took all her energy to climb the stairs, shaky as she was now from the awareness that had suddenly spring up between them.

She locked her bedroom door, trying to keep herself in as much as keep Baron Selkirk out. This never happened to her. She could not recall ever being so sexually carried away over so little. Over a mere glance. A few seconds more, and they could have been having sex on the kitchen counter.

She sighed, throwing herself back into the bed. It would have extremely pleasurable, she was absolutely sure. She and Baron set off sparks together. If she hadn't been so sick this morning, who knew what might have happened in the elevator?

Oh, lord. Poor Caz. No matter how sexy Baron Selkirk was, and how much Addie was attracted to the idea of getting to know him a whole bunch better, she could not let Caz down. She must return to Jackson Hole in time to testify.

*****

Baron held his breath until she turned on the landing and was out of sight. Finally, he exhaled. What the hell just happened? They'd gone from arguing to sizing each other up as potential lovers. He knew the signs. What about his offer to carry her up to bed? Sheer madness. She was smart to turn him down, because he would have been in that bed with her, making love to her despite her fragile condition. From the look she'd given him, she'd considered it.

He policed the kitchen, stowing the plate and the pitcher of tea, and turning off the lights. His pulse was still jumping. Feisty Addie did that to him, turned him into a tyrant who wouldn't hear of letting her leave. Were all men pigs? Offering to carry her to bed. Right. Genius. He was lucky she hadn't laughed in his face. She'd gone pink instead. He'd seen the flush that rose in her cheeks. Her hands had trembled a bit, too. She'd known what he wanted. Maybe she'd wanted it, too.

The nightgown under her robe had hidden her major assets modestly, but had ended above her knees, showing off nicely shaped legs and pretty toes with pink polish. He shoved his feet into his boots, and flung on a coat. He needed to walk this off. Women knew how to make the most of their power over men. Here he was salivating over Addie, a near stranger, because he'd seen her toes. Too bad Miss Betty hadn't found Addie a granny gown that reached the floor and hid those toes. Whatever a granny gown was.

# Chapter 4

Addie woke again when the sun was up. Someone was knocking. Miss Betty's voice came from outside the bedroom door.

"Would you unlock this door, child, so I can give you your clothes and check on you?"

She dashed over and turned the bolt, swinging the door open.

"Sorry."

Miss Betty eyed her. "You must have been awake in the middle of the night. I checked on you up to midnight."

"I woke around two and went and had some of your cookies. They were wonderful."

"Well, thank you. I wasn't sure if the boss had made off with them. He does like sweet things." As she spoke, Miss Betty bustled about the room, pulling up the shades and letting in strong sunlight, then setting the bed to rights.

"Where is he now?" Addie asked.

"Oh, over at the ranch manager's office, givin' orders, I expect." Miss Betty motioned that Addie should sit on the bed.

After checking her forehead and taking her pulse, the older woman nodded. "Short of a complete physical, I'd say you're back to normal."

"I feel fine now."

"Good. I'll leave you to get showered and dressed. Unless you suspect you might need help?" Miss Betty asked, cocking her head.

Addie shook her head. "I'm all better."

"Glad to hear it. Come down when you're ready and I'll make you some breakfast."

After Miss Betty left, Addie searched through the neatly folded clothes. No cell phone. She'd have to call from their land line, later. She'd forgotten to look for a kitchen phone last night. Along with a clock, an old-fashioned land line was a missing accessory to the guest room. Baron probably didn't get many guests lacking cell phones.

*****

Over a large breakfast of eggs, bacon, and waffles, Addie pumped Miss Betty for information. "How big is this ranch?" Addie was seated at the kitchen table same as the night before, but now sunlight poured in from windows and a door leading outside. The old lady had a sitcom on her wall-mounted television, but she'd muted the sound.

"Over 100,000 acres."

"That's huge. Did Baron grow up here?"

"All three kids. He and his little sister, Tess. They have a brother, Jesse Dwayne. Call him JD. He was seriously wounded in the Iraq war."

"That's too bad."

"Better than dying, I'd say, but not much. Just about broke their mama and papa. They decided to go live near him at the VA hospital. Over to Cheyenne. Don't know when or if he'll recover enough to lead a normal life. Maybe they'll come back some day. Maybe not."

"What about Baron? What did he do?"

"He came home, and took up running the ranch. Guess he could have persuaded his parents to sell up and be done with it, but he didn't. Maybe he came here to heal a bit himself."

Addie nodded. "Makes sense."

"Mind you, I don't know how he feels," Miss Betty said. "I'm only guessin'."

"You know the family well? You've worked here a long time?"

"Nineteen years. Came when the kids was little, and helped take care of them and give their mama a rest."

"What's the sister like?"

"Tess? She's a firecracker. Always into things. Never afraid of trouble. She's flyin' in tomorrow."

"Flying in?"

"We've got an airstrip beyond the rise. Usually, Baron travels by plane."

"He drove to Jackson Hole."

"He took a little time off before Tess's visit. She's comin' with her friend, Paula, to stay for a while. Paula always flirts with Baron."

"Does he like her?"

"Not the way you mean. Known her since she was just a kid friend of Tess's from boarding school."

"What does Tess do?"

"Lately? Run wild, is my opinion."

"That's not a nice thing to say about my sister, even if it is true." Baron's voice preceded him. He came in from outside after carefully wiping his boots on the doormat.

"Tess is solid," Miss Betty said. "You'll meet her day after tomorrow. And Paula."

Baron winced. "Her, too."

"Don't you like this Paula?" Addie asked.

"'Course he does," Miss Betty said. "He's just gunshy from all the women who make a play for him. Including Paula, ever since she growed up. She wasn't like that as a young girl."

"Can we not talk about Paula?" Baron asked.

Miss Betty was enjoying herself. "Now, boss, you know it's a fact that Paula chased you around the mistletoe last Christmas until you tore it all down."

He rubbed the back of his neck. "She's a nice girl, but she can be a pain."

"That's why he went to Jackson Hole, to bring a woman back to be his girlfriend."

"To pretend to be," Baron said, flushing a little. "Someone to take the heat off me."

"You went to Jackson Hole looking for a woman?" Addie asked, laughing.

"Found one, didn't I?" he said. He raised an eyebrow at her.

She stopped in mid-laugh. "Pity you dragged me back.

Why don't you just man up and tell this Paula to stop chasing you?"

"Because she's Tess's best friend," he replied.

"If only you had an actress here to play the part of your girlfriend," Addie goaded him.

"An actress," Miss Betty repeated. "Of course. Boss, why don't you let Paula think Addie here is your new girlfriend?"

Addie suppressed a grin. Little did they know that she had the acting chops to pull off such a masquerade.

"I'm not afraid of Paula," Baron said. "Let's talk about something else."

Miss Betty was having too much fun teasing Baron in front of Addie. "Appears to me you could use a pretty gal like Addie here to run interference."

"If you're done embarrassing me, I'll go to my office now." He stalked out.

Miss Betty guffawed.

Addie chuckled. "Is he really worried about this Paula's visit?"

Miss Betty eyed her. "Not anymore, I don't think."

"Because I'm here to be a decoy?"

"Yep. Appears to me he found a woman."

"Despite his wrong ideas about me."

"You'd know best about those," the older woman said with a smile. "Got my own thoughts about what the boss's ideas are."

Time to change the subject. "You said something about Baron returning to the ranch after his brother was wounded."

"Baron's a geologist by trade."

"Not a rancher?"

Miss Betty hung up her dish towel. "They all was raised to know how to run this ranch, but JD was most interested."

"He left, too, to serve in the military?"

"Their papa wanted Baron to run the ranch. JD didn't see a place for himself here."

"Even though Baron wasn't here? This is confusing."

"Baron was all over the world."

Not the country boy after all. That changed her view of him rather drastically. He wasn't the insular type as she'd supposed. "Was coming back here difficult for him?"

"Made him more bossy."

"How could you tell?" Addie asked, deadpan.

The older woman let out a laugh. "Good one. He's always been responsible. Now he's even more so."

"Which reminds me," Addie looked around for a phone. "I ought to call home. Don't you have a phone in this kitchen?"

The old lady got an uncomfortable expression on her face. Her nervous glance at the wall revealed a phone wall plate, but no phone. "Well, uh…"

"Did Baron remove them so I couldn't call anyone?"

"It sure looks that way," the older woman muttered.

"All of them, you figure, so there's no point me looking for one in another room?" Addie asked.

Miss Betty nodded.

"Did you find my cell phone in my jeans pocket?"

Miss Betty shook her head. "No. If I had, I would have returned it, no matter what the boss says."

Addie sighed.

Miss Betty continued. "If I had one of those phones myself, I'd lend it to you. Never saw any need for one before now."

Addie stood up and patted Miss Betty's shoulder. The older woman clearly felt bad about the situation. "Point the way to his office. Guess I'll have to confront him about whether I'm a guest here or a prisoner."

Miss Betty took her to the back hall and pointed to the last door on the right.

"Good luck, girl."

Addie wasn't afraid to argue with Baron about the phone. What Addie didn't like was being alone with Baron in a small room. Given the raging chemistry between them last night, anything could happen. Although that might have been a fluke.

She knocked on the door and, on his invitation, went in. It was a classic ranch office, all dark hardwoods. The story of the west was emblazoned on every wall. Pictures of cattle. Horses. Land. Her eyes went to the land line phone on his desk.

Baron stood up from his desk and gestured for her to have a seat. Those old-fashioned manners again. She sat. He remained standing.

She had to crane her neck to address him. "I seem to have lost my cell phone, possibly in your SUV. I'd like to use your land line to make a couple of calls."

"I don't think that's a good idea."

She tamped down on her instant exasperation. "Explain to me how keeping my friends from starting a statewide police hunt for me is a bad idea?"

"Who would those friends be?"

She crossed her arms. "None of your business. I have no obligation to tell you anything about my personal life."

"If you won't explain, then I'll use my own judgment. No phone calls until I'm sure you're off the drugs."

"I took a sinus medication. I had a bad reaction. End of story."

"So you say." He picked up a paper from his desk, as if dismissing her.

"Did you know somebody who did drugs?" she asked. "Did some woman let you down?"

"We're not talking about me." He retrieved his hat. "Right now I have to check on my crew."

"I need to make a phone call. Otherwise, I'll be a missing person and there will be trouble," she said.

"What kind of trouble?" He eyed her as if he knew she was already trouble.

She was safe enough telling him part of it. "A media circus. I'm a known person in Jackson Hole. I can't just vanish."

He dismissed her explanation. "I've got things to do this morning. Stay in the house and rest."

He motioned for her to leave his office first then locked the door behind them. He tipped his hat and left her staring after him as he strode out a side exit.

No way was she kicking her heels in the house. She'd never been an indoors kind of girl. She'd explore the ranch. Maybe she'd find a phone, too.

She took a hat from a rack by the front door. In her jeans and boots, she was already clad correctly for a ranch. True to her heart, she went directly to the stable. Horses whinnied softly as she walked by. She talked to each of them, but kept walking, enjoying the familiar, pungent smells of hay, horse, and manure. At the other end the open door led to a corral. Within it was a magnificent white stallion.

"Oh, you beauty," she cooed.

"You be careful there, miss," came a voice from behind her. "He ain't been trained." A wizened older man walked up to her. He wore ranch gear, jeans, boots, a long-sleeved shirt, and a hat, which he doffed respectfully. "Hoot Hawkins is my name."

"I'm Addie" She offered her hand. "Are you the trainer?"

"Don't have one right now. Lookin' for one." He gazed at the horse and shook his head.

"Why do you have a horse and no trainer?"

"Boss's sister, Tess, sent this fire breather. Saw him being mistreated. Bought him from the owner and shipped him here."

"Good for her."

"That girl has a kind heart. Knowed her since she was a tiny little thing."

"Now you have an abused horse that needs help," she said, eyeing the stallion with sympathy. He raced around the corral, obviously excited at being watched, but nervous, too.

Hoot sighed. "That I do. You know a trainer?"

"I train all the horses on my ranch myself."

Hoot looked impressed. "I'd give you a tryout, but I heard you was sick. Plannin' to stay here a while?"

"No." She cast the stallion a look of regret. "I'd love to work with him."

"We got some safe horses here. I'll show 'em to you. You can pick the one you like best, in case you and the boss go for a ride later."

She took up his offer, although she would not hold her breath waiting for Baron to invite her for a ride. He might think she'd attempt to gallop away to freedom.

At first Hoot carefully kept her back from the horses. Once he realized she knew how to behave, he let her pet them and talk quietly to them. She whiled away some time admiring the animals, who were all in tip-top condition. The stalls were in excellent shape, too. The tack room held a good selection of the best quality tack. And a wall phone.

"Would you mind if I use this?" she asked.

"Jest dial your number. I got to go check on somethin'." With a tip of his hat, he was gone.

She wasted no time calling her ranch manager. After giving Trudy a seriously censored version of events, she said, "Capture this number on Caller ID. Give my friend Caz a call. Although he isn't answering his phone right now. Okay. Go into town with a note. Deliver it to the hotel and make sure they promise to take it to him. Tell Caz I promise I will be there as scheduled with—"

The phone was yanked out of her hands. "She won't be making that deal anytime soon, you scum," Baron shouted into the receiver and hung up.

"What did you do?" she cried. "Now he'll think I'm in trouble."

"You won't call your dealer again. No deliveries to that hotel, either."

She pressed her lips together and inhaled, trying to calm herself. "You've got it all wrong."

"You can't be trusted." He took her wrist and began to drag her bodily from the tack room. She resisted, digging in her heels.

"Let go of me. You have no right."

Instead of releasing her, he pulled her into his arms. He bent an angry look on her. "I won't let you hurt yourself again."

She struggled, but he only held her closer.

"The moment my back is turned, you're trying to get hooked up again. You'll kill yourself. You've got to stop."

"No," she said. "No."

He wasn't listening. Was he even seeing her? Some powerful emotion drove him, but did it relate to her or someone else?

Her body ignited from the feel of his rubbing against her. She stopped struggling. She couldn't fight him anymore. At this dangerous moment, when she least needed to feel lust, she did. Her body wanted to sink into his, to feel her softness against his hardness. She wasn't afraid of Baron, a man who stood when a woman entered a room. She feared her feminine desire to yield to him sexually as a means of defusing his anger.

Their eyes clashed. Could he see how much she wanted him? He saw something, for he lowered his head toward her. Desperately, she held up her palm between them. "Don't you dare kiss me."

"You want me," he ground out.

"You're acting like a cave man." She turned her head away.

Would he touch her against her will? His hot breath fluttered her hair. Would he force her?

Neither moved.

He stepped back and let her go. "I'm sorry. I was out of line."

She backed up against a stall and stared at him, breathing hard, fighting desire. Perhaps he felt lust, too, but he was fighting another strong emotion. She shook her head to clear it. "This isn't about me at all, is it? Who in your life has a drug problem? Where is that person?"

He pulled the tack room door shut and locked it. Then he turned without a word and stalked off.

"Wait a minute," she cried. "You can't just manhandle me and walk away. I demand an explanation of your domineering behavior."

Hoot reentered the stable at that instant. "Was you wantin' to ride?" He registered the expressions on their faces, and turned as Baron strode past him. "No, I'm guessin' not."

"I'd like to ride," she said, deliberately loud enough for Baron to hear even as he stalked away.

"That okay with you, boss?"

"Yes," came a growl from the departing figure. "Tomorrow. Not today."

Hoot shrugged. "Gotcha." He turned back to face Addie, still standing in the stable. With an apologetic look on his face, he said, "Maybe take it easy today? Sit on the porch and relax."

She shook off the spell she'd been under. "All right," she said. "I'll get out of your hair."

That man turned her inside out. She'd never felt so

instantly physically attracted to anyone. Even stranger, she'd been hot for him despite his anger at her. Why had her brain short-circuited that way? Was it some kind of atavistic feminine instinct to calm a powerful, angry male?

What was eating Baron? Why did he leap to the conclusion that she'd phoned a drug connection? Who did he know who had a drug problem?

She should find a way to escape. Being attracted to a man who yelled at her and manhandled her was bad. She was at risk.

She'd like to ride the horses, and train the wild stallion. Would she still be here tomorrow? Not if she found a way to escape.

# Chapter 5

Baron ate his lunch under Miss Betty's disapproving glare. He'd arrived in a bad temper, grumbling about the roundup, the weather, the ranch hands, the horse he'd been riding, and anything else that came to mind. Miss Betty had listened and then put him straight. Trust her to know how to do it. He was lucky she hadn't clipped him one with her wooden spoon.

"Don't come into my kitchen throwin' your weight around, thinkin' you're the big time rancher." Her exasperation with him was easy to read in her stance, both hands on her hips and one hand holding the wooden spoon that had taught him a few lessons when he was a boy.

"I'm in charge now," he said. "They should do roundup the way I want them to."

"This is your first year back on the ranch, boy. Thinkin' you know better than ranch hands who been doin' roundup here since before you was born is foolish."

"I want it done my way," was his stubborn reply. He gulped his ice tea.

Miss Betty banged a pot hard on the gas stove. "You got Hoot, with forty years experience, and you don't listen to his advice."

"He wants me to do it the same old way."

"'Course he does. Take it easy this first time," she said, turning back and pointing the spoon at him. "Get the hands used to you bein' the boss."

"That's not how it's done in the rest of the world."

"A ranch lives or dies based on its hands stayin' year after year, bein' loyal. You make them miserable, they'll leave, and then where will you be?"

"I'll hire new hands."

"Look around you, boy. We're in the middle of nowhere." She banged the pot on the burner again. He winced at the clash of steel on iron.

"You ever talked to your daddy about how hard it is to find good workers and keep them?" She shook her head, disgusted.

He'd called his father for advice on how to run things a few times in the beginning. Dad shook him off, concerned only with JD. Tried again only last month. Nothing. It was as if his father didn't care what happened with the ranch, or with Baron. Only with JD.

"As for how you been treatin' that girl you brought here—"

Miss Betty's aggrieved tone brought him back to where he was. "I don't want to hear it," he said.

"You gonna listen to me. What you gone and done this time, boy?" she asked, her manner now concerned instead of angry. "That girl's mopin' about the house. What did I tell you about keepin' your hands to yourself?"

He flushed.

"Aha. I knowed it," she exclaimed.

***

Addie sat on the front porch of the ranch house all the rest of the morning, having discreetly ascertained that none of the ranch vehicles' keys were on the hooks in the kitchen. Baron must have removed them, in case she thought to steal a car and drive to freedom.

Miss Betty brought her lunch on a tray.

"I'm sorry to cause you more work," Addie said, leaping up to help the older woman place the tray on a wicker side table. "I could have come to the kitchen."

"Lot of hot air in there today. Best keep away until there's a cooling wind."

Miss Betty meant Baron. He must still be angry, if anger truly was what that scene in the tack room was all about.

"I made a phone call out at the tack room. He didn't approve," Addie said.

Miss Betty clucked.

Addie continued, "I couldn't let my people think I'd vanished. Is there something in Baron's past I should know about? He keeps accusing me of being a drug addict."

Miss Betty sat down on a nearby rattan rocker, grimacing as she settled in, as if she was tired. "Not my story to tell. He had a bad experience with someone close to him."

"That's quite a teaser."

"Best I can do."

"I'll ask him directly, then."

Miss Betty stared at Addie. "When lunch is done I like to watch my old TV shows. I especially like *Golden Days*," the older woman said with a significant look. "You remind me of that little Jelleff girl on the show."

Addie gulped and choked. The lemonade she'd sipped almost went the wrong way. Was Miss Betty onto her? "Uh…how so?"

Miss Betty set the rocker in motion. "Smart little girl. Sticks up for herself when that brother of hers gets her in trouble."

Caz. He'd played her mischievous brother when they were kids on TV.

"Don't you think they were both following a script?" Addie asked.

Miss Betty shot her a shrewd look. "Maybe so, but I like that little girl. Character shines through. If that girl needed help, I'd offer it." The housekeeper stood up. "I'll collect the tray later. I imagine the weather's cleared up in my kitchen by now." She went back into the house, leaving Addie to ponder the meaning of her words.

Nothing was quite as it seemed here at the ranch. Baron Selkirk had a serious bee in his bonnet about drugs. Miss Betty affected a super loyal attitude, presenting herself as the type who did not interfere with her boss's actions. Yet she'd strongly hinted that she knew who Addie was. Had been. That if Addie needed to escape this ranch, Miss Betty would provide assistance. There was a way home, if Addie understood right. She exhaled, finally relaxing for the first time all day. She was not a prisoner.

Probably she should take her opportunity to leave right now, but it would be convenient to hide out here for a couple of days and avoid the tabloid reporters. Get to know Baron better.

Where had that idea come from?

The cave man scene in the stable was troubling. He'd come on hot and heavy without her consent. Worse, she'd liked being touched by him that way. Liked it far too much when he'd crushed her against his chest and nearly ravished a kiss from her. Ravished. Oh, my. Then he'd backed off and even apologized for grabbing her. He hadn't forced a kiss on her, either, despite what he must have felt in her yielding body.

Enough. She'd freshen up, then go down to the stable and see if Hoot would let her work with that white stallion.

\*\*\*

Hoot shooed Addie back to the house again, "Boss's orders." No more horses for her today. It was odd not being with horses. She'd spent almost every waking hour of every day for the past four years with the animals.

Unwilling to sit around anymore, she rooted through the closet in the guest room and came up a tee shirt and shorts, and an old pair of sneakers that fit well enough when coupled with her thick socks. After liberally applying sunscreen she'd found in the medicine cabinet, she retrieved her borrowed hat and exited the house by the front door.

First, she paced off the area in front of the house. After walking back and forth, counting her steps, she'd done a mile. No ill effects. No weakness. She'd recovered.

Next she paced around the house. A neat vegetable garden

was positioned near the kitchen door. Its lushness contrasted sharply with the parched aspect of the back yard behind the center of the house. A large pool deck was surrounded by desert plants spaced well apart. The pool was Olympic size, and a small white gazebo beyond it served as a pleasant design element and focal point for the pool area. The gazebo complemented the classic architecture of the ranch house. It evoked a turn-of-the-19th-century feel despite the presence of the in-ground pool and a batch of chaises and tables with umbrellas. The lack of a conventional lawn or flower borders showed some concern for the desert environment. Ornamental grasses dotted the yard and there were patches of sturdy native plants, but no big, water-slurping borders of lush annuals and perennials. In this part of the state, water was too precious to waste on flowers. Yet the Selkirks had an outdoor pool. It looked to be a recent addition. Maybe for the sake of the injured brother? But he was in Cheyenne, hundreds of miles away.

The ranch house was connected to a detached three-car garage by a covered walkway, again with the gingerbread feel of the gazebo. The exit directly from Baron's office was through that walkway. A four-wheeler sat next to it. No keys in the ignition.

She checked out several outbuildings, too. Most were locked and she could only guess at their purpose. She cast a longing eye at the stable, the place she'd be happy to explore all over again. Off limits.

The sun was hot, but she needed a run. Without a pedometer or familiar markers, she'd go for time, not distance.

She was about to set off down the drive when Miss Betty appeared at the kitchen door.

"You'd best come inside and take a rest, girl."

"I'm about to go for a jog."

The old lady frowned. "Give yourself some time to get used to the desert. 'Tweren't many hours ago you were nigh unto helpless."

If Baron had stood there and forbidden Addie, she would have taken off like a shot. She owed Miss Betty more courtesy. "I did a mile walk in front of the house and I was fine."

"That's good." Miss Betty shaded her eyes in the glare of the hot sun. "You trainin' for a marathon? 'Cause otherwise, a mile is enough when less than twenty-four hours ago you couldn't walk by yourself."

"Baron wouldn't let me." He'd carried her in his powerful arms. The memory of feeling so light and so secure in Baron's clasp made her breasts rise with a deep inhalation.

Miss Betty huffed out a breath, signaling her annoyance. "You gonna argue all day, and me with a cake in the oven that needs tendin'? You plannin' to be a patient again, or you gonna be sensible?"

Addie kicked the gravel with her toe. "Okay, I give. You're right."

She walked up the two steps, and went through the screen door Miss Betty held open for her.

"Now you're bein' smart, girl. You take it easy the rest of today. Get a nap. Read a book."

"Yes, ma'am."

"I mean it. Don't go runnin' up the stairs or chinnin'

yourself at every doorframe. Get more rest." She gave Addie a stern, no-nonsense look.

With that, Miss Betty went to check on her oven. Addie slowly walked upstairs, finding she was more tired than she'd expected. She decided to take a shower and wash off all the sunscreen and the dust she'd kicked up outside.

A few minutes later she was clean and dressed in a white cotton camp shirt and a pair of tan slacks from the closet. She was at loose ends again. The shower had revived her. Napping held no appeal. At home, she always kept busy. She trained her horses until she was physically exhausted and they were sick of the sight of her.

She'd go visit that white stallion. Visit, nothing more. He looked like a wonderful horse.

This time around, she left the house by the front door, avoiding Miss Betty's sharp eyes, and went directly to the corral, skirting Baron's order that she stay away from the stables. She also dodged Hoot and his adherence to keeping her away from what she loved the most.

She approached the corral and stood by the wooden fence. The white stallion got curious. He came over to check her out.

"Oh, you're a beauty, aren't you?" she said in a low-pitched, affectionate tone of voice. "Yes, you're a good horse, a very good horse," she continued. "I'll bet you'd like it if I rubbed your neck. Wouldn't you, boy?"

The stallion snorted and danced away in a show of power. He bucked up and down and raced around the corral. She didn't move. A few minutes later, his curiosity impelled him to come stand by her again. She spoke to him softly, praising him.

"That was so much fun. You're such a handsome boy. I'm even more interesting, because I'm going to help you be a very happy horse again. Yes, I am."

She talked in that vein every time the stallion came near her. It was tempting to touch the beautiful horse. The stallion offered by moving his shiny head close to her, but she didn't know his tricks. He might be a biter, and she didn't have her training stick. Anyway, this visit was all about showing the horse who was the boss in this relationship. By making herself available but not too available, she trained him to want her. Too bad it didn't work on men.

Where did that thought come from? She'd never had any difficulty attracting men. Her show biz glamour did the trick even when the polish and poise she'd developed as a child actor failed her. Which it seldom did. Truth was, she received far more male attention than she wanted, and all because she'd been on a TV show years ago.

The stallion approached.

"You're a very good horse, a very good horse. We'll take a ride tomorrow, maybe."

The stallion raced away.

No, her problem with men was that they saw her as an actress, and as nothing else. Like Baron seeing her as a drug addict and nothing else. Maybe stubborn, simplistic thinking was a trait all males suffered from.

The stallion tried not to show his curiosity, but he couldn't resist checking her out again.

"You're a wonderful, wonderful horse, and together we're going to bring out the best in you," she cooed.

***

Two hours of preliminary training went by in a flash. The white stallion would make an excellent riding horse or even a competitor. He'd been trained, but something had happened to scare him into behaving badly. He wouldn't require much remedial effort.

All the while she trained the stallion, her thoughts about Baron kept churning. When he appeared next to her at the corral fence, she didn't jump.

"I told you to stay away from my stable today," he said in a gravelly tone from behind her.

She smelled horses on him, and smoke. Leather. Manly smells. "I'm not at the stable," she said, still watching the stallion.

He ignored the technicality. "I specifically ordered you not to come back here today."

She finally glanced at him. "You ordered? You're acting like a prison warden."

"You're a guest, but you were sick. Or so you claim," he said, eyeing her with open suspicion.

She curbed her impatience. "Haven't you ever taken even one pill that made you loopy against your will?"

"No. Never." His glare was uncompromising. "I don't do drugs and I don't allow them on this ranch."

"I don't do drugs either," she said. She glared back at him.

"Why are you here at the corral?" Baron demanded.

"I'm training your stallion, getting him used to humans."

He frowned. "You went inside the fence?"

"I wouldn't do that without permission."

"Why should I give you permission?"

She blew out an exasperated breath. "Because I'm a horse trainer."

"Pull the other one." He looked her over, missing none of her female assets, making her want to squirm from his slow, appreciative inventory. "You're far too beautiful."

"You're kidding."

"What are you? A dancer at the casino? A swim instructor at the hotel?"

"Why would you think that?" She cocked her head at him.

"You have an air about you. Poise," he said, his hands resting on his belt as he looked her over.

"That's an astute observation," she replied, impressed in spite of herself. Although she wasn't about to tell him about her show biz past, somehow he'd made a connection. "Why is my appearance relevant to my ability to train a horse?"

"The only horse trainers I've ever met were wizened old things. You don't look like a horse trainer to me," he said.

"I can't possibly be a horse trainer because I don't look the part?" She started laughing.

"What's so funny?"

"I don't look the part." She couldn't stop the gales of laughter.

"You've been out in the hot sun far too long. Miss Betty told you to rest. I'm taking you back to the house." He took hold of her upper arm and began to march her toward the ranch house.

"Stop," she said, sobering up. She pulled against his strong grip. He immediately released her, but now they were face to face, almost touching. Their breaths mingled and then slowed. She stared into his chestnut eyes, seeking something, she didn't know what. His gaze was equally intent. He answered her without words, and then he looked at her lips. She stopped breathing. He leaned in a few more inches and pressed his mouth against hers.

Her body slammed against his, as if propelled. Her arms encircled his neck. His large hands grasped her waist and pulled her tighter against him. Her softness crushed against his hardness. The kiss deepened. The world spun.

Then the stallion nickered and Addie fell out of heaven. She backed away from Baron, one hand to her mouth. What had she let her captor do to her? What had she done?

"No," he said, seeming to grope for words, as if he, too, was dazed by the force of their kisses. "What?"

She forced herself to remember he'd been trying to drag her off. Otherwise, she would leap back into his arms for more. She had to stop thinking about his kisses.

"What's his name?" she asked.

"Who?"

"The stallion."

"Whitey." Baron looked at the horse, which was circling the corral again. "He's plain crazy," he said. "You're nuts to think you can civilize him."

"You are completely wrong about this horse," she said. Turning back to the enclosure, she called the stallion. "Whitey. Whitey. Come here, boy."

"He won't come," Baron said.

The white stallion pranced up to where Addie stood at the rail.

"Whitey," she cooed. "I've just learned your name. Whitey. It's a beautiful name. Whitey. You are a beautiful and good horse, Whitey."

\*\*\*

Baron was seized by a sudden wish that she would talk to him in that loving tone of voice. It had been a long time since he'd heard a woman address anyone in such softly affectionate accents.

That kiss. The feel of her in his embrace. She was all woman. He wanted her.

"Bye, bye for now, Whitey," she said. She turned and walked away from the corral, her blonde hair swinging under her cowgirl hat matching the sway of her hips. The horse nickered, but she didn't turn back. "Bye, bye, Whitey," she repeated in a firm vice. Then she walked on.

Baron caught up with her and they walked together. How had she turned the tables on him again? He'd been about to drag her back to his house and yell at her for disobeying orders. Make more of a fool of himself, in fact. Instead, they'd caught fire from a mere touch. He'd wanted to devour her. She'd given back to him with equal intensity. They would be amazing together, if he could coax her into his bed.

Despite her response to him, she'd recovered first. She'd argued with him, as everybody seemed to these days. Then she'd demonstrated her horse-training ability, which was impressive.

How could such a gorgeous, womanly woman already have that rank stallion eating out of her hand? Everybody said it would take months to civilize him. They were wrong. If Addie stayed here, he bet she could do it in a week.

He'd like Addie to stay for much more than a week, but what was his excuse? She wasn't on drugs after all. Miss Betty had told him in no uncertain terms that he was barking up the wrong tree. He'd leapt to a false conclusion about Addie during their very first meeting. Instead of volunteering to take her home, he'd compounded his error by refusing, and then by yelling at her when she'd phoned her people. He'd behaved like an idiot. Not to mention grabbing her and practically losing control this morning and just now, too. He kept wanting to put his hands on her. Wanting to touch that soft pink flesh.

When he got close to her, an elemental part of him took over. His body started making his decisions for him. He drew a heavy breath. He ought to regain his self-control and act civilized, stop giving Addie Smith good cause to leave here and never see him again. How could he keep her here long enough so she'd change her mind about him? Could he offer her the job of training Whitey? Was that enough of an enticement?

Was she truly well enough? The white stallion was a dangerous horse. Would Addie be safe trying to train him? He couldn't let her risk her life. He must protect her.

***

Addie was very conscious of Baron walking beside her as she made her way past the stable toward the ranch house. He was a strong, virile man. She'd been lucky so far that his scruples and hers had dragged them back from giving in completely to the attraction that sizzled between them. They'd come very close just now. Her knees felt weak.

He was deep in thought as they walked together. Perhaps he'd changed his mind about her and now would be willing to help her get back home? She only had a few days before the trial began. She'd promised Caz. He needed her.

"I have to return to Jackson Hole soon."

She must have said it out loud, for he replied, "What's your big hurry?"

"Someone is depending on me."

"Are you engaged? Do you have a kid? What?"

She let him see her exasperation. "Isn't it a little late to ask that? You kissed me."

"You're not wearing a wedding ring," he said, picking up her left hand and stroking her ring finger with his large middle finger. He looked at her with challenge in his eyes. "You kissed me back."

She withdrew her hand, slowly, and stepped a few feet away from his tempting body for good measure. His touch was too potent. Her hand tingled where he'd stroked her. She wanted him to stroke other parts of her. She walked toward the house with renewed speed, but Baron kept pace with her.

"Well?" he asked again.

Her mouth quirked in an almost smile. "Not married. No kids."

"Then how about staying here for a while?"

She stopped walking. "Suddenly I'm not a prisoner? You

finally believe I'm not a drug addict?"

He grimaced, looking uncomfortable. "It wasn't that unreasonable an assumption. You were in bad shape in the hotel. That episode with the guy at the suite door insisting I leave before he'd open up was weird. Then you climbed into a stranger's car and were out cold for hours. You couldn't walk straight."

"I'll never take another allergy pill again in my life," she said, her right hand raised in swearing position. "Can we forget that?"

"I'll take it under advisement," he said, cracking a smile that made her insides melt. "Stay here as a guest. You could train Whitey."

"Okay, but only for a few days." She shook her head, fighting the tempting idea. "I have an important appointment in Jackson Hole, one that I can't miss."

"What kind of appointment?"

She gave him a searching look, wondering how he would take the truth, all of it. "I have to testify in court. A friend of mine is in trouble."

Baron's expression shut down. "A friend? Or a drug dealer?"

She threw up her hands in frustration and slewed around, looking anywhere but at Baron. He had a one-track mind, and it always led to drugs. Just as well she hadn't tried to explain Caz, and Leslie, and the shooting, or the D.A.'s ambition to make a name for himself.

"Did I say anything about drugs?" she asked.

He shook his head, as if to clear it. "I won't help you keep a drug dealer out of jail."

She put her hands on her hips, facing him. "Are you back to thinking I'm in cahoots with a drug dealer?"

"In cahoots?" He smiled. "What a wild west word. From your way of speaking I don't think you were raised in Wyoming."

"Stop trying to distract me. Do you still suspect me of something illegal?"

Baron didn't answer directly. "Who'd you call?"

"What?"

"Who did you call from the tack room this morning?" Baron braced his hands on his hips and stared down at her from his impressive height, his whole pose demanding.

"None of your business," she said, not giving an inch.

"You were arranging a delivery. What was it?"

She stared up at his frowning face. What flight of fancy was he onto now? "You misheard me, Baron."

"No. You called your supplier. Or your dealer. Or maybe it was your creepy boyfriend."

"I do not have a— No. Why should I tell you anything? How dare you make assumptions about my life?" She turned away. She resumed the short walk to the house, only now she was nearly running.

"Slow down," he said. "We need to talk some more."

"No way. You don't listen."

She was practically sprinting when she got to the ranch house kitchen.

Miss Betty looked up as she burst in. "What on earth?"

"Talk some sense into him. He's gone around the bend."

Baron pounded into the kitchen only a step behind her, but she didn't stop. She raced out of the room and upstairs to her bedroom. She locked the door from the inside.

# Chapter 6

In the kitchen, Miss Betty stopped Baron from following Addie by moving between him and the doorway to the main hall.

"Whoa, there, cowboy. What's your hurry?"

"Let me by."

"Leave her be." Miss Betty put both flour-covered hands on his forearms. "A girl needs to be alone sometimes."

"I have to talk to her."

"Simmer down."

She nudged him toward the kitchen table. He sat. The noise of her television show was a familiar undercurrent in her kitchen. She poured him a glass of iced tea and pushed a small plate of muffins nearer.

"Now what's this all about, boy?"

He took a sip from his glass and blew out a breath. "She used the phone in the tack room this morning, but she won't tell me who she called."

Miss Betty looked at him as if he was about ten years old. "Why should she?"

"What do you mean?"

"You don't own this girl," Miss Betty reminded him. "You found her, but she don't belong to you."

He said nothing for a minute. Then he let out a deep breath. He wanted Addie to belong to him. He thought of her as already belonging to him. "Maybe so."

"She won't confide in you if you keep pushin' her away with your suspicions."

"I don't believe she's a drug addict. Not anymore."

"Well, I should say not." She turned back to the stove and fiddled with a pot. Then she faced him again. "Another couple of girls you don't own are showing up here tomorrow. Tess and Paula. Don't you be gettin' down on Tess, you hear?"

"She needs to straighten up and get on with her life."

Miss Betty bent a stern look on him. "Says the pot about the kettle. You're in a holdin' pattern and you know it."

"No, I am not."

"Then where are the women? You're young, healthy, good-lookin', and you're rich. Yet you go to a resort and come back with a woman you all but abducted. That ain't the normal way to get a gal."

He didn't have a comeback. The last few years he hadn't found any woman who interested him for more than an evening. Addie interested him mightily. He wanted to know everything about her, but she wouldn't spill. Stubborn woman.

"Message received. I'm going to my office." He stood and walked out of the room.

\*\*\*

Addie didn't leave her bedroom the rest of the afternoon. She lay on the guest room bed and thought about Baron Selkirk. What was his problem? Why was he constantly accusing her of being involved with drugs? Or had he now shifted to jealousy because she had dared to call another man? Was that it? Did Baron think he owned her?

A shiver went through her. Owned by Baron Selkirk. Why was the thought so exciting? Her breasts felt swollen and achy. Her mouth was dry. Her stomach was clenched. Her whole body remembered how it felt to be in his arms. He was strong, demanding, masterful.

She groaned in frustration and turned on her side. Baron had taken her captive, although now he claimed she was a guest. She could not succumb to the atavistic female sexual thrill of being forced to yield to him, of being possessed against her will rather than giving herself freely. The kiss hadn't been forced on her. It had been mutual. But still, she'd arrived at this ranch under duress, and her position still wasn't stable. She must remember that when she was tempted to succumb.

What did her attraction to Baron say about the state of her love life? Did she need or want a lover right now, when her life was such a mess again? A lover who lived hundreds of miles from her little ranch? Although she liked the isolation here, especially as a break from the media frenzy involving Caz.

Her love life was barren and had been for a long time. The last man to breach her defenses had eventually revealed his acting ambitions and that had ended it. Before him? College boyfriends. High school boyfriends. Important at the time only. The last two men she'd dated had wanted her for her supposed Hollywood connections.

To get away from the aggravation of men who wanted to use her, she'd stopped dating men who knew she'd been an actor. Jackson Hole had been pretty good to her for the past two years. No one had recognized her all grown up at age twenty-four and not wearing glamour makeup and clothing. She'd blended in. Now the shooting had spoiled it all. The tabloids had dragged out her past as a child actor, and put the sleaziest spin on it possible. According to them, she'd run away from a wild life in Hollywood and yet was having an equally wild affair with Caz. Long distance.

Did Baron recognize her? Was that why he thought she was involved with drugs, because he assumed everyone involved with Hollywood was? An extreme notion even though he'd made no sign that he'd ever watched her sitcom. Unless he'd seen it recently in the ranch kitchen.

For a few minutes outside, he'd finally seemed to back off from his half-baked notions. Then something got him even more wound up. What had she said to fan the flames of his suspicions all over again?

\*\*\*

Miss Betty knocked and called through the door, "Addie, are you all right in there?"

She sat up. She'd been soundly asleep. She stumbled to the door and unlocked it. "Sorry."

"Dinner time. The boss went out. Said not to expect him back."

"Please don't tell me he drove to Jackson Hole for dinner. Not when I need to get back there," Addie said, hugging herself.

"He went over the hill to the mess house, where the ranch hands eat. To play poker."

"That's better." It wasn't, not really. She wanted to keep talking to Baron, but not have him blow up at her with his crazy suspicions.

She spent a quiet evening alone after Miss Betty said goodnight and headed for her separate apartment. The housekeeper reminded her they'd be getting more company tomorrow.

Addie turned on the television in the den and found the sleazy channel Caz had watched in his hotel suite. Sure enough, his story was mentioned as a teaser before each commercial break. Then, finally, the story devoted to him began. It was appalling. In footage from her old sitcom, she and Caz bickered at their kitchen table. Their TV mom watched over them lovingly. Then their TV dad came home from work and they made wiseacre remarks to him.

He'd been a brilliant man but his sitcom role was to play a bumbling idiot. He'd died of a drug overdose a few years after the show ended. The tabloid TV announcer made much of the man's death, wondering aloud if the actors on the show were under a curse.

"Will Caz Cassidy's missing lover appear when the trial begins?" The TV displayed grainy footage of Addie taken at her ranch. "Where is Adrienne Jelleff hiding? Keep tuned, or log on. In Wyoming, we'll have live testimony in real time, as it happens."

She switched off the television. After her testimony was broadcast, she could never live anonymously in Jackson Hole again. She might as well sell and move on.

"What are you doing?" Baron entered the room. His expression was hard to decipher. A mixture of tiredness and anger, perhaps.

She indicated the blank TV screen with a wave of her hand. "How was your poker game?"

"Miss Betty told you, huh?" He put his hands on his hips. "Waste of time."

"Isn't playing poker with your employees somewhat unethical?"

"They don't see themselves as working for me. They follow my dad's orders." He said it as if it made him angry.

She made a face. "I'm confused. I thought you ran this ranch."

He flopped down on the couch next to her, his long legs stretching out to tangle with hers. "I'm in charge now, but certain people…" He slanted a sideways look at her. "…don't do as I say."

"Do your employees refuse to follow your orders?" She sat up straighter and edged a little farther from him on the couch.

Baron put one arm along the back of the couch. "The ranch hands say, 'Your daddy does it different'."

One large finger touched a strand of her hair, played with it. She repressed a shiver. She suddenly was very conscious of all her most feminine body parts, which Baron was eyeing hungrily. Her nipples peaked and a pang shot from them to her lower body.

He'd told her something important about himself, but her thoughts were so scattered. He was too close.

"Addie," he breathed, and then he kissed her. His tongue quickly entered her mouth and she forgot about air, except to sigh. His arms pressed her against him. Her breasts swelled and nestled against his large chest. When he began to open her blouse, she regained her mind and stopped him.

"No," she said.

Baron sat up, his expression angry. "I've heard that word too many times today."

"I'm not your employee. I can say no if I want to." She wrapped her arms around her body, signaling that he should back off, trying to keep her unruly response to him in check.

He rubbed the back of his neck, then sat up on the couch and grabbed the remote. "Message received." He turned the set on again.

She breathed a sigh of relief. As a bonus, the celebrity gossip show wasn't on anymore.

Baron clicked the channels up and down until he found the cop show Caz starred in. "Want to watch this with me?" he asked.

"I don't usually watch cop shows," she claimed.

"This one is okay. Cassidy's quirky but cool."

Still, she hesitated.

"It's our chance to be in the same room for an hour without arguing," he urged.

"Since you put it that way." She settled into the couch. Baron was right. When had they spent even one hour together peacefully? The only time was when she was asleep in his SUV. Otherwise, their relationship was a total contest of wills versus bodies. He issued orders and attempted to control her every action, and she resisted. He had the upper hand because she was stuck on his isolated ranch. She promised herself that if he didn't offer to take her home over the next couple of days, she would take Miss Betty up on the implied offer to help her leave.

Caz was his usual charming self as the episode unfolded. In between car chases and handcuffing perps, he romanced his female partner, plus a girl-of-the-week.

"They've been building this storyline all year," Baron said.

"They'll kill off the girlfriend, which will make him turn to his partner for consolation. Plus, they can tragically kill her, too, for added drama at the season's end."

"You know a lot about television. Is watching what you do after a long day of talking to horses?"

Oops. She took a veteran's interest in television, paying attention the minute details the public never noticed. Better not suggest to Baron that she had a Hollywood connection. "I only watch while I use my treadmill," she said.

"Is that how you stay in such fantastic shape?" His eyes roamed her body.

She ignored his meaning, trying to dial it down. "Limiting my movements to what won't frighten a nervous animal can be frustrating. The treadmill burns it off."

"You don't have family to care for?"

She gave him a look that said she was onto his attempt to weasel personal information out of her. "I believe I told you I am not married and I have no children."

"You did, but you were plenty cranky when you said so," he said with a half smile.

"That's because you were prying into my personal life."

"I'm interested. That's all," he said with a righteous air.

She wasn't buying, but she didn't challenge him on it. The ads were over and Caz was romancing his latest lady. It got hot and heavy. Addie made to edge off the couch before Baron got ideas again. "I think I'll leave."

"Don't you want to see what happens next?"

"It's television. They'll cut to one of those annoying bedroom scenes with people improbably clutching sheets to cover themselves."

He chuckled. "True. Television's not realistic."

She stood, but he pulled her down again, onto his lap. He shut the television, and tossed the remote away.

"What are you doing?" she said, struggling to regain her balance.

"What does it look like? Why don't you relax?"

She stared at him. He looked as if he intended to kiss her. Or more.

"Since when do you and I relax with each other?" she asked.

"If you'd just follow my lead, we'd have something." He put one large hand on her neck, and stroked up to her jawline.

She should move. She should resist. But once again she was mesmerized. His touch sent her nerves zinging. She waited for what he would do next.

His hand went to the back of her neck and pulled her head

down to meet his lips.

Sensation engulfed her. In a dim corner of her mind, she remembered she should resist, but that voice was tiny. Every other part of her was shouting for more. More of his lips, more of his tongue, more of his hands on her as he turned and positioned her under him on the couch. His fingers found their way under her blouse and her bra. When they touched her nipples, she jerked.

"You're so responsive," he muttered. "So hot." He opened her bra and caressed her breasts, sending tingles throughout her body.

Her body throbbed with the need to let him take more. Her will to oppose him was draining out of her. If she let this happen, she would be lost. So would he if he seduced his too-willing captive.

Captive. She arched up and started fighting. "No. Don't. Get off me."

He pulled back and she surged off the couch, panting, trying to cover herself. "This can't happen."

He stood up and moved to take her into his arms again. "Why not?" he asked. "You want it as much as I do."

"Not this way," she insisted, backing away. "I'm not the totally expendable girl-of-the-week."

He frowned. "I never said you were."

"We've got too much chemistry," she said. "Any little thing sets us off."

"Chemistry's a problem?" There was a smile in his voice and a knowing look on his face. She flushed inside at the implication that they would be hot together. That was the problem.

"You abducted me and are holding me prisoner." She backed farther away from him. Her blouse still revealed her breasts and their engorged nipples. He glanced at them desirously. Her nipples reacted by tightening. Her desire for him was a painful ache, but she must fight it. She wrapped her arms around her middle. "My body doesn't rule me, Baron. My mind does. You don't decide for me, and I don't let my body decide for me, either."

She didn't look at his crotch, which she was sure also showed the evidence of how eager he was. They'd come too close to having sex. She still panted for him. His breathing was heavy, too. In the silence of the room, her breaths were loud. Too loud and too suggestive. She'd fall back into his arms any second now unless she riled him up enough to back off.

"I am your prisoner, not a guest on vacation."

"I like the sound of that," he replied, taking a step closer.

She rolled her eyes. "I hope you're joking. I'm not into kinky."

"You don't want to play games?" he asked lightly. He pulled her into contact with his body and began to kiss her again.

"No. I can't. I—promised him…" She sighed.

He dropped his hands from her shoulders. "What man did you promise?"

"I won't tell you," she cried. "I won't." She fled, afraid he touch her again and cause her body to give in despite all her fine principles.

# Chapter 7

Addie spent the rest of the night fighting her body's need to go to Baron and finish what they'd started. In her dreams, she and Baron were naked in bed together, driving each other crazy. She begged him to come to her, but he never did. More than once, she woke up throbbing, unfulfilled, needing Baron. Luckily she had no idea where his bedroom was, because she might have given in and gone to him. Her body was on high alert, demanding sexual fulfillment. It totally could not be trusted.

In the morning she was up early and decided to go for a run. Not for good health, but to scourge her body out of its ridiculous ache for Baron Selkirk. She wasn't the cold shower type, but the morning air was brisk. It helped.

She began to enjoy herself as soon as she built up some speed. The physical frustration ebbed. She ran toward the highway, although running her maximum distance wouldn't even get her to the front gate. She wasn't a marathoner. Without a pedometer or familiar markers, she had to guess where to turn back. She would use her exhaustion as her guide.

A few minutes in, she felt calmer. She was ready to stop punishing herself for last night. She spied a good turning point, the top of the rise. As she made a final sprint for it, the noise of a vehicle's tires and motor came from behind her. She moved over to the edge of the drive and turned slightly, prepared to wave as it went by. Instead, Baron's SUV screeched to a halt directly in front of her, churning up dust. He slammed out and got in her face.

"Are you out of your mind?" he yelled.

Tempted though she was to jog around him, she stopped. She leaned over, bracing her hands on her thighs, to catch her breath.

"If you're trying to run away, it won't work," he said. "The highway is still five miles away."

She straightened up. "You have a problem with me exercising?"

"You're still weak. You should rest."

"Then what was last night about? Do you think sex is restful?"

As he reared back and color flooded his cheeks, she held up a hand. "No, don't bother to answer." She put her hands on her hips, fighting the temptation to poke him in the chest for emphasis. "Back off, big macho cowboy. I'm not a dainty little blossom."

"You can't run away from this ranch. There's nothing around for miles."

"I'm well aware that you want me to be your prisoner here." She kicked the dust with the toe of her sneaker, and glared at him. He looked too good in the morning sunlight.

His hair glinted from the moisture of his morning shower. His face, clean shaven, looked carved from stone by a master sculptor. His body was to die for, broad-shouldered and narrow-waisted.

She pushed those thoughts away. "I'm exercising so my frustration doesn't become intolerable. You got a problem with that?"

He said nothing, just stared at her. Was he remembering how she looked last night with her blouse hanging open? How she sounded when he touched her? Her memory of those moments likely was in her eyes for him to see.

She tried again, "I'm not that other person," she said. "I'm not a drug user who spends her days looking for another hit."

"Get in the SUV. I'll drive you back."

He held the door open, a courteous gesture if she didn't know he was likely to pick her up again and stuff her bodily inside if she balked. She didn't want him touching her, not when she was so sensitive to his touch.

"I can run back to the house. I was about to turn anyway," she said.

He adjusted his hat to shield his eyes from the morning sun. "Miss Smith, would you please get inside?" he asked. "It's too cold to argue out here, and Miss Betty has breakfast ready."

She relaxed. She couldn't help smiling. "A classic case of 'I'm cold, so you should get warmer?' Okay, since you're asking nicely." She hopped into the SUV and let him close her door for her. It was warm inside.

Once back at the wheel, Baron wasn't in a hurry to start the vehicle again. He looked at her. "You confound me. When we met, you were unable to stand upright without assistance. When you walked away, you were unsteady."

She nodded.

"Now you're acting as if you have too much energy and have to burn it off somehow."

"I'm usually busy all day. A sedentary lifestyle doesn't do it for me," she said.

He leaned back in his seat. "I was wrong about you."

"I was sick at that hotel. You didn't know that was a one-off for me." She shrugged.

"Why are you making excuses for me? I've been a jerk."

"I can think of a few reasons, but I wouldn't want you to get too puffed up." Then she rolled her eyes at her slip of the tongue. "I didn't mean…"

Baron grinned at her. "Like the way I was last night."

Better not talk or think about last night.

"What is this all about, anyway?" she asked. "Who in your life has a drug problem?"

"Haven't you wondered why I don't have a girlfriend?"

"Not much, considering how many times you've tried to kiss me," she replied, smirking.

"And more," he reminded her, looking at her lips as if he wanted to kiss her again, right now.

Memories of last night arced between them. Her body began to throb again. She must redirect this conversation to something safer. "Don't try to distract me. You were appealing to my pity by saying you don't have a girlfriend?"

"I did," he grimaced. "In college. We were together for

years. She got the acting bug. Dropped out and took off for Los Angeles."

Addie held her breath. L.A. This story was not likely to end well.

He braced one arm on the steering wheel. "I went out to visit her. She'd gotten a few bit parts. She claimed she was doing well. The next time I visited, she was different."

Addie recited the next act, knowing it happened to hundreds of young hopefuls who went to Hollywood looking for fame and fortune. "The constant rejections wore her down, so she got involved with the wrong crowd."

Baron nodded. "Soon she was doing drugs. I could tell right away. She started living with some strange guy, a real creep. She wouldn't leave him, probably because he was her supplier."

Addie nodded, seeing the pain on his face as he remembered. His hands clenched on the steering wheel. His eyes stared ahead, looking at nothing.

After a minute, he said, "I saw her once more. She was so thin she was skeletal. She claimed her big break was right around the corner. I could tell she was using big time. I tried to stage an intervention, but she told me she'd married the creepy boyfriend. She showed me a cheap ring. Said I had no right to tell her how to live. I had to walk away."

He was silent so long she prompted him. "Then?"

"She died within a year. Burned herself out with the drugs." He rubbed his face, as if trying to wipe the memory from his mind.

"Tragic," she said.

Baron looked at her, his eyes burning. "When I met you, you reminded me of her. That same combination of vulnerability and dignity."

"You couldn't save her, and I don't need saving," she said, in a quiet voice. Baron was clearly in the past.

"I thought I was over my failure. Those feelings rose up and bit me when I saw you," he said.

"Because my situation looked similar."

"My frustrations about her transferred to you. Maybe other frustrations, too."

Feeling her way, she said, "Yesterday, our conversation seemed to take a turn for the worse when I said I have to get back to Jackson Hole for an appointment. What do I have to do to convince you that I am not your old girlfriend?"

"Stay here."

"I can't. I have a commitment."

"Is it personal?" His eyes narrowed as he stared at her, as if he was trying to peer into her soul.

"You could say so. I won't talk about it."

"I'll get you to talk eventually."

She eyed him. "Is that a threat or a promise?"

"It's a promise." He leaned over, cupping her chin with his hand. "I always keep my promises."

Her breath caught. Something warm and knowing in his eyes reached out to her. She began to relax and soften inside. Her lips parted. He lowered his head and kissed her.

It was a tender kiss, full of promise. His lips caressed hers, and she responded, enjoying the soft feel of flesh on flesh. When she felt the questing tip of his tongue, she surrendered completely. When he finally withdrew, she sighed.

His hand smoothed her cheek. He kissed her again, and she wrapped her arms around him.

A few minutes later, they came up for air.

"Whoa," she said.

He smiled and turned the key in the ignition. "Time for breakfast."

She sat in a daze during the short ride back. Where were they headed? She'd give him points for playing fair today. He didn't press his advantage by trying to interrogate her after softening her up with his kisses. What came next?

Stubborn man. Eventually, she would tell him everything, but not when he still refused to help her get back to Jackson Hole.

As he pulled up in front of the ranch house, she asked "May I train Whitey?"

"Are you really a horse trainer?" He looked unconvinced.

"Certified."

He still appeared doubtful.

"Whatever I do someone else can build on," she said. "I don't train horses to be one-person animals."

"Tess and Paula will arrive in a few hours."

She shrugged. Their imminent arrival didn't mean much to her, though it appeared to weigh heavily on Baron. "In a couple of hours I can help Whitey get substantially more calmed down, which will be good for him and for whoever deals with him in the future."

"All right. Don't overtire yourself."

She resisted rolling her eyes, although his concern for her

health touched her. He dropped her off at the house and continued on over the rise to where the ranch hands lived.

***

She rushed through breakfast and then quickly changed into her jeans and boots. This was turning into a great day. She headed outside to spend the morning with Whitey. The sky was blue, the temperature had risen to a comfortable level, and she would be with a horse. Life was good.

A few minutes later she found a training stick in the tack room—whose wall phone had mysteriously vanished. That man. He never gave up. He wanted her to stay here. If he wasn't so darned bossy, she'd like to stay. His insistence brought out her own determination to go.

Miss Betty called Baron "boss," but Addie did not intend to be bossed around. Some women might feel secure with a man who wanted to rule their every hour. Not her. She wanted to make her own choices.

If she ever was in a serious permanent relationship, then she'd have to compromise some. That's what all the old married couples claimed made marriage work, compromise. Maybe it was true, but she'd never had an opportunity to test the need for compromise in a healthy relationship. She'd never had a serious relationship that was healthy. How twisted was it that she even considered what was between her and Baron a relationship? He'd abducted her. He was keeping her a prisoner on his ranch. It was a fancy ranch and a mostly pleasant form of imprisonment, but she was not free.

She'd never been so strung out by desire before. Every time he touched her, she wanted to rip her clothes off and offer herself to him. She wanted to yield. She must keep fighting. She couldn't allow him to run her life or trap her into going against her principles because of a sex thing. How could she live with herself if she let Caz down?

She should stop thinking about Baron. It only made her hotter for him.

Once she saw Whitey, all other thoughts fled. She concentrated solely on the stallion. She started again by standing outside the corral, cooing in low tones, encouraging the stallion to come to her side. She didn't touch him until she was in the corral and had more space to move herself and move him.

Once inside, she clucked and made gestures with the training stick, urging Whitey to move back to give her room. When Whitey moved as she urged him to move, she praised him.

"There's a good boy. There's a wonderful stallion."

Whitey sidled up to her and she stroked his neck just under his mane, praising him all the while. Her training had taught her that happy enzymes were created by this stroking that imitated what a horse's mother would do.

Every correct action Whitey took was rewarded with soft, encouraging words, and strokes on his neck. She never touched him with the training stick. She used it as a pointer, an extension of her arm.

She did push him around. She made him understand that she was the leader, and if she wanted to be in a spot, he must yield and retreat. She spoke her commands in a calm voice, a firm but friendly voice, and always in a low tone. When he did as directed, she softened her voice and cooed.

After an hour or two, maybe more, Hoot's raspy tones came from outside the corral.

"Miss Addie, they want you up at the house."

She gave Whitey more strokes as she moved toward the gate.

"Okay, time for me to go now," she cooed. "Now, back up," she commanded, indicating with her stick that the stallion should give her room. He obeyed.

Hoot opened the gate and she slipped out. She turned around immediately and praised Whitey.

"What a good horse you are. Yes, you're a very good horse." Whitey moved to get his head over the rail. She stroked him some more.

"All right. Yes, you are a very good horse. Goodbye for now."

"I'll be. Never seen anythin' like it." Hoot escorted her through the stable.

"Why did you all think Whitey was a rank one? He behaved himself with me."

"He arrived kickin' and screamin', that's why. Rolling his eyes and carryin' on somethin' fierce."

She'd arrived at the ranch in much the same condition as Whitey. "He probably got transported insensitively, and panicked on being dumped into a new situation."

"Could be. You're a miracle worker to calm him down so quick."

Hoot said goodbye and she walked the final steps to the

ranch house. She'd calmed down on the ranch much quicker than Whitey had, and with less effort by anyone. Baron wasn't a woman whisperer, but his innate good manners and his clear sense of honor made her trust him and relax. Still, like Whitey, she remained cautious. Although Baron had not mistreated her so far, he had come close. He'd manhandled her. And he had yet to help her return to Jackson Hole.

Caz felt he would pay serious consequences if she didn't testify. She would lose his friendship and be vilified in the tabloid press, too. She didn't care about the tabloids, but hurting Caz was something she didn't want to do.

She walked into the ranch kitchen and found Miss Betty putting food on the table.

"Do I have time to clean up?"

"Be quick about it. Biscuits comin' out in a minute."

"Biscuits. Yum. Be right back." She flew upstairs and took a fast shower. Then she donned more of the casual clothes from the bureau in her room.

***

Baron was in his office, looking at geology jobs online, when he heard Miss Betty's first call that lunch was on the table. He rubbed his face. His morning had started off great, kissing Addie. The rest of today, not so much.

Arguing with the ranch hands over details of the roundup wasn't what he wanted to do with his life. The conference in Jackson Hole had given him leads for new geology projects with interesting employers, but he couldn't take any of them, dammit. He had to stay here and run the ranch.

Run the ranch. Not him. The ranch hands ran the oiled machine his father had created. Dad had a genius for organization and leadership. He'd laid out every aspect of the ranch work in a clear system. Many of the men had been here since Baron was a boy, and they were loyal to his dad's system. Now that much of the work utilized four-wheelers and computer chips, ranch hands didn't wear out physically, so guys didn't give up early. Even Hoot, who'd taken some bad falls off horses in his rodeo days, was fully able to do his job by riding around in the Jeep or one of the four-wheelers. Baron had tried to get the old man to retire, but settled for letting him run the stables and act as his sub-manager. Not that there was much to do in the stables with Addie training that stallion. Or anywhere else on the ranch, with the hands following his father's systems and not listening to his ideas.

The ranch didn't need Baron, but he was stuck here anyway, until JD got better, or until their parents decided to move back or sell up. Whenever that happened. JD had returned from the war a year ago. The outlook for his recovery and return to civilian life still wasn't good.

Meanwhile, the days of Baron's own life went by, and at age twenty-nine, the work he'd spent years training to do, geology, not ranching, was forbidden to him. Family duty was nothing but frustration.

"Boy, you eatin' lunch, or what?" Miss Betty called again.

"Coming."

***

Addie sat down at the table, and a few seconds later Baron arrived, his mind clearly somewhere not pleasant. After a casual glance at Addie, his gaze sharpened. His eyes examined her clothes. He frowned.

Suddenly conscious of how much skin the cami and shorts revealed, she asked, "Is there something wrong with my clothes? You're giving me the stink eye."

"Not much clothing in evidence," he said, scowling.

"Last night I got the distinct impression you liked that," she replied.

"What?" Miss Betty shrieked.

"All I did was kiss her," Baron told his housekeeper.

"Excuse me, but there was a lot of touching going on, too, Mister-Holier-Than-Thou. There'd have been more if I hadn't escaped."

Baron's face flushed red. "You responded. Don't deny it. I could have had you if I'd pressed."

"How dare you?" Addie cringed mentally at the show they were putting on in front of Miss Betty, but couldn't stop. "This isn't about my clothes. It's about you being frustrated because I keep saying no."

"Set yourself down and concentrate on lunch," Miss Betty advised.

Addie took an angry turn around the room. "I've lost my appetite," she replied. "Excuse me."

She left the kitchen.

Back in her room, her stomach growled. Breakfast was a long time ago. She stared at her body in the mirror on the bathroom door. There was nothing provocative about her shorts and cami. Why was a frown from Baron Selkirk enough to set her off? She'd jumped down his throat. Was it because they'd come so close to making love last night, but been frustrated? Yet they'd been okay this morning. This morning had been sweet. Why had she blown up at him?

She talked to her reflection. "You will return to the kitchen and eat lunch like a civilized person. You'll stop baiting Baron and you'll ignore him if he happens to frown instead of smile at you."

She sank down on the closed toilet seat. Miss Betty had worked hard to provide hot food. It wasn't her fault that Baron and Addie had a volatile relationship. She shouldn't have embarrassed Baron in front of the housekeeper. She'd overreacted. Maybe they both were on edge because they'd come close, so close last night.

She slipped into the kitchen a few minutes later. The television was on, and Miss Betty was alone at the table, eating.

"I apologize for causing a scene," Addie said. "May I still have lunch?"

"Sit down, girl. 'Twas the boss that started the trouble."

Addie helped herself to biscuits that were still a little warm. "All he did was frown at me. I took offense awfully quickly."

"That you did." Miss Betty took a bite of her biscuit.

"I don't understand why he thought I wasn't properly clothed."

Miss Betty didn't roll her eyes, but she looked as if she might. "'Tain't the clothes, it's the girl inside. When Paula wore that outfit, the boss ignored her completely."

"I was trying to spare you the smell of horses."

The older woman made a gesture with one hand, pushing aside the topic of the quarrel. "When he brought you here, I told the boy not to take liberties, but from what you said, he has."

Now it was Addie's turn to feel her face redden. "I'm afraid Baron told the truth about last night. I kissed him back."

"Do tell," Miss Betty said. "Well, you sure put a bee in his bonnet just now. He took off for parts unknown after you stalked out."

"Did I truly stalk out?" Addie asked, bemused by the image.

"Yes, you did. It was like a movie," Miss Betty said. She continued with a gleam in her eye, "Or an episode of a sitcom."

Addie went still. "Television is very fake."

"You two sure have been actin' like you was in a TV show. I watch a lot of 'em while I cook. I'm an expert." Miss Betty smiled.

"What's next in the script?" Addie asked, trying to look only a little bit interested.

"Tess and Paula arrive to complicate matters," said the older woman with satisfaction. "Tonight I'm servin' dinner in the dining room. Should be quite a scene with Paula hangin' all over Baron, and him eyein' you like a prime piece of meat he wants to chew on, and Tess lookin' daggers at all of you."

# Chapter 8

Baron took the big SUV over to the air strip. Tess and Paula should be arriving in a few minutes. Anyway, he needed to cool off after almost letting his personal frustrations make a hash of things with Addie.

She didn't have to blow up at him like that. She was driving him crazy. She had a body that just wouldn't quit, and she ignored it completely, and ignored him, too. Except when she didn't, like last night. Last night, she'd been eager. She'd wanted him, but she held him off because of the abduction thing. He should apologize to her and take her home. Then they could start over. No, she'd never give him the time of day again and, anyway, he supposedly was needed here. Addie wasn't the only prisoner on this ranch, not by a long shot.

He got out of the SUV and stared at the sky to the east, where the plane would appear. When he was a kid, he'd liked living here in the middle of nowhere. Now, thinking of all the things he was missing, he wanted to hop in his own plane and take off, never to return. If he at least knew when his tour of ranch duty would end, he could make plans for his future.

Tess would probably arrive drunk as usual. He'd tried to get her to stop drinking, but she insisted it was the only way she could cope. She never tried to talk about her misery to their parents. She was thoroughly cowed by them. As for himself, he should call or visit and have it out, but then his mother would cry, and Dad would get that look. Better to keep doing his duty, and say nothing.

***

Addie would enjoy returning to the corral to work some more with Whitey, but it would be too much for the horse too soon. She never pushed horses. She gave them time to adjust.

She'd taken her run this morning and that was enough serious exercise. Maybe she'd go for a swim. There was that pool in the back yard. She could imagine Baron's expression if she swam wearing one of the tiny bikinis from the guest room bureau. Her own fury if he made more comments about her borrowed clothing. They were at each other's throats because of their sexual frustration. How had they managed a sweet kiss in his Jeep this morning? Every other scene ended in hot feelings, whether desire or anger. Usually both.

She wandered the main living room of the house, picking up framed photos of Baron, Tess, and JD together. They were a handsome group. JD had sandy hair and a cocky grin, and stood a bit shorter than Baron. The three smiled broadly through a series of informal snaps and school portraits as little kids, then teenagers, and finally college age. Growing up here must have been fun.

Baron didn't smile much now. Was it because he resented having to take up the burden of family duty and move back to the ranch, or was it the reason for the move? JD's injuries sounded pretty bad.

If Baron was touchy, maybe she shouldn't take it so personally. Although she'd felt very personally frustrated last night when their desire had nearly overcome them.

If she lived on a big ranch like this, she'd be busy all day training one horse after another. She'd never get bored.

A swim might work off some of her restless energy, the restlessness that came from being cut off from her normal volume of work as well as her usual channels of communication and entertainment. No cell phone. No tablet or laptop.

There must be a way. The wall phone was still missing from the kitchen, but Miss Betty had a desktop computer in a niche just beyond the passage to Baron's office. Why hadn't Addie noticed it before? The boss's idea of a nice perk, no doubt, in case Miss Betty wanted to look up a recipe online or make a spreadsheet listing the supplies in her pantry. Although it was unlikely she did either. Baron was a generous employer. Miss Betty had all the latest and fanciest appliances, too. Yet what the elderly housekeeper appeared to take the most pleasure in was her small wall-mounted television. If Miss Betty was in the kitchen, sitcoms were playing.

Addie asked permission before sitting down to open the computer. Miss Betty, done with her kitchen chores, had hauled out a duster with intent. "Go ahead, child. I don't know how to work that thing and I don't plan to learn."

Addie reached the Internet without needing a password, a precaution hardly necessary out here in the middle of nowhere. She searched for the latest on Caz and the upcoming trial. There it was: "TV Star Love Triangle Shooting Confession," with a photo of Caz. The clickbait headline led only to speculation about Caz's love life, no direct quotes from him. The trial had been moved up and jury selection had already begun. She only had a couple more days to hide out.

A teaser headline named her, too: "Former TV Child Star Vanishes." Someone had taken a photo of her in the parking lot. It was fuzzy, but it caught her running. The article speculated that she'd left Jackson Hole because of her guilty long-term affair with Caz.

Right. An affair they'd been carrying on long-distance somehow since the show went off the air when she was twelve years old. Caz was a very immature thirteen at the time, not interested in girls at all. Four years ago, they'd reconnected as friends during a planning session for a made-for-TV reunion movie that thankfully never got made. By then Caz was already on the road to grown-up fame, looking for a pal who didn't want anything from him. Addie fit the bill. At the time she was still hanging on in L.A., trying to live down her TV career.

Two years later, she finally gave up and moved out of state. It was just their rotten luck that Leslie Tone jealously followed Caz when he came to visit her. What a mess.

Did Caz ever check his e-mail? Her ranch manager did. She quickly created a new free e-mail account and sent a message saying she was all right, naming where she was staying and with whom. To Caz she sent a more discreet message in case it was intercepted. She merely said she was out of town, avoiding the media. She promised she would return to Jackson Hole on the day her testimony was required, and asked for updates. She also mentioned that she'd lost her cell phone.

What else could she do? A live phone call via the computer would have been possible, except she didn't know Caz's number by heart. That came from only using her cell's capture technology to file and access it in her address list. He had to change his number often. Caz's Twitter identity had been hacked so many times they never communicated that way. She sent her manager a request, but would have to wait to see if he answered. She closed the computer.

Addie wandered the house again, checking out her bedroom for a few minutes, but unable to stay there. Miss Betty had returned to the kitchen. No need to crowd her.

"Addie," came the older woman's voice.

"Yes, ma'am?"

"Come on back here a moment, will you?"

When Addie walked into the kitchen to her horror, the television was playing an episode of *Golden Days*. Her openmouthed reaction betrayed her.

Miss Betty nodded. "Thought I recognized you."

"Please don't say anything to anyone."

"Why are you so far from home?"

"Trying to escape my childhood." Addie flung herself down at the kitchen table. "I was never that girl. I was acting, reciting lines someone else wrote. It wasn't me. I wasn't a wiseacre or a brat."

"That little thing for sure never put a stallion through his paces," Miss Betty cackled. "Hoot told me what you been up to at the corral. You're a long way from Hollywood. How come?"

Addie smiled a little. "I was a child, doing what my family wanted of me. Lots of Hollywood kids act, so I didn't feel weird or different."

"But?"

"As I grew up, I realized I didn't have what it takes to keep on with an acting career. Not as an adult."

"You had trouble with grabby men?" Miss Betty asked, showing concern.

"Maybe a little." She shrugged. "More the petty lies, the smiling faces and then the stabs in the back."

"Shame on them."

Addie stood up, back to feeling restless. "I hate even talking about it. That time is over for me. My life is elsewhere."

The older woman nodded. "I won't tell. I won't watch the show anymore while you're here, neither."

"I appreciate it. I don't want my past to always influence my present," Addie said.

The loud sound of an airplane came from outside. They both looked up, although there was nothing to see. That must be Baron's sister and her friend, Paula.

"Oh, goodness, here they are. I've got to finish up." Miss Betty cried, and began fussing with food preparation again.

Addie walked through to the front of the house and stepped out on the porch. A small plane flew beyond the rise to the working part of the ranch, and vanished. The landing strip must be there.

Miss Betty had suggested there was something up with Tess. As for Paula, Addie couldn't wait to meet Baron's unwanted suitor. Seeing him squirm would be fun.

A few minutes later, Baron's SUV came over the rise. It drew up at the house just as Miss Betty emerged.

"Welcome, welcome," she cried.

The doors opened and a tall, dark-haired young woman jumped out and embraced Miss Betty. "Hi, Miss B. You look great." She kissed Miss Betty on the cheek, then strode over to Addie. A wave of liquor smell wafted between them. She offered her hand. "I'm Tess Selkirk."

"Nice to meet you."

At her words, the other young woman looked up from greeting Miss Betty. Paula Barton introduced herself.

"Are you Baron's new girlfriend?" She made "girlfriend" sound like a disease.

"Addie Smith," she replied. "Did you come from very far away?"

Paula shared a glance with Tess. "Didn't Baron tell you? We were over in Cheyenne, where JD is."

"My other brother," Tess said. "JD lives at the VA Hospital. He was seriously wounded in Iraq."

"How's the boy doing?" Miss Betty asked.

"The doctors say he'll never walk again," Tess replied with a throb in her voice. "Mom and Dad are totally freaked out."

"He'll walk," Paula said. "He's the most stubborn man I know. More stubborn even than you, Baron," she said, flirting with him with her eyes.

Baron hefted luggage and avoided looking directly at Paula.

"You two packed enough for a month. What gives?"

Tess said, "Carry our bags or don't, your choice. Don't complain."

Addie's eyes widened. He made no reply, just took the cases into the house.

Paula called after him in a sweet voice, "You have permission to heft all my luggage, Baron." She touched Tess on the arm, but Tess shook her off.

"No, don't tell me to be nice. I've made nice to JD for days and days, and it does no good. He takes it as permission to walk all over me."

"He can't walk yet."

Tess grimaced. "Mom and Dad keep telling me to be even sweeter, as if that will change anything. He's bitter and mean and I hate it," she finished.

Baron stood in the front hall. "You coming in, or you planning to stay outside in the sun like an idiot?"

Addie raised an eyebrow. She aimed a general comment at the others. "I'm going to the stables. See you all later." She took off before anyone could object.

***

"The stables?" Tess asked Baron, as she and Paula entered the house. "Why would your girlfriend go to the stables?"

Baron looked at Addie's swiftly retreating figure and wished he could take off, too. Being around his half-drunken sister had tensed him up already. In the shape she was in, she turned anything into a fight.

"She probably wants to avoid our squabbling." A bright idea struck him. "Matter of fact, I promised I'd go riding with her this afternoon. I took your bags upstairs to your rooms. Why don't you two get settled, have the snack Miss Betty prepared, and I'll see you at dinner?"

Tess looked frustrated, but his suggestion was too reasonable for her to flatly reject it. Paula was probably thinking of something flirty to say. He seized his opportunity and took off after Addie.

He caught up with her inside the stables. "You have to rescue me from my evil sister."

Addie bent a disbelieving look on him. "How am I supposed to do that?"

"Go for a ride with me. I'll show you the whole place."

"I hear you've got 100,000 acres. It could take hours."

"Yep." The tightness in his chest loosened as he contemplated hours alone with Addie.

"Now I get it." Her face showed mock disapproval. "You want to avoid your guests. Your guests who have just arrived and probably expect you to spend time with them." She put her hands on her hips. "You are nowhere near an ideal host, I must say."

"Sure I am," he said, grinning down at her. "I abduct the good-looking ones and ignore the ones I already know. Makes perfect sense."

She began to giggle. He took her arm gently to lead her to a stall. Mistake. The electricity arced between them.

He gave in to impulse. He pushed her up against a stall and kissed her. When she wrapped her arms around his chest and kissed him back, he groaned at the intense pleasure. Her arms around him felt incredible. Her soft breasts pressed into his chest as her softer lips caressed his. He ached to have her completely.

He finally pulled back. "What is it with you and me? I didn't mean to do that, I swear. All I did was touch your arm."

She'd leaned back in his arms, and her reddened lips were half-opened with desire. An invitation if ever he'd seen one. Why was he talking? He kissed them again. This time, she moaned. Her fingers restlessly stroked his back, which suddenly was highly sensitive.

He came up for air and pressed her against him. "If we don't saddle the horses this instant, we'll be having sex up against this wooden wall."

Her eyes went wide with shock, whether from his words or their actions. She visibly shook off the spell and turned to find a saddle on a sawhorse.

He groaned as she leaned over and her tempting backside wiggled in front of him. He leaned in and pulled her hips against his. He put his hands on her rounded breasts. She collapsed against him for a moment. Then she stiffened.

"We've got to stop," she said, holding very still.

He turned her in his arms and kissed her ears and her eyebrows while his hands roamed her breasts. Her eyes were somnolent. She was near to yielding. He put one leg between hers and pulled her tighter against him.

She gave a shuddering sigh. "We must stop." she repeated. "Please. No more."

"Why not?"

"Your sister will come looking for you. Or Hoot will wander in."

He muttered a heartfelt curse. He took a deep breath, fighting every atom of his body. Finally, common sense returned. He hefted the saddle and walked toward a stall.

"This one's a mare. You'll like her."

They made quick work of saddling up and riding out of the main compound.

\*\*\*

Addie suspected Baron planned to find a more private place and persuade her to make love. He had a look of determination in his eyes. This manly man saw no barriers between them, despite his role as her captor. He'd have his way with her, or at least give it another try.

Her traitorous body was eager, but right now, she needed a break. She wanted to think things over. "Show me where those recalcitrant ranch hands live," she said.

He led them over the rise, where they had a good view of the bunkhouse, two small homes, three small house trailers, and a building with a large wraparound porch. He pointed to it.

Not a soul was visible anywhere. "Where is everybody?" she asked.

"At roundup."

"Why aren't you?"

"They don't need me. I put in an appearance a couple of times a day, and then let them get on with it."

Something in his voice made her cock her head and study his face. "I thought roundup was this intense, hands-on experience, like the grape harvest if you own a vineyard."

"Could be." His eyes showed no eagerness.

"You're not deeply engaged in ranching, are you?" she asked.

"I'm a geologist. I was called back from a promising shale deposit to run the ranch. Ever since JD came home wounded."

"But you're still here. How long has it been?"

"A year."

The bleakness in his tone told her everything she needed to know about Baron's real attitude toward ranching.

He made a visible effort to shut away his emotions. He looked over at her. "If you want to be part of a classic cattle roundup, tomorrow we're all doing the last bit of it together, for fun. It's cattle ranching lite."

As their horses continued their slow pace, he pointed out the purpose of each building, and answered her questions about the ranch employees. "I'll pay you for training Whitey."

She shook her head. "Not necessary. Anyway, I have to return to Jackson Hole in a few days."

"You could stay." There was unspoken promise in his suggestion.

Would he still want her once he knew who she was? She sighed. The tabloids would paint her with a dirty brush from now on. Because Baron's past experience with Hollywood was seedy and tragic, wouldn't he believe the worst about her past in tinsel town? He'd believed the worst about her bad reaction to the allergy pill.

Their mounts ambled along a well-marked path that took them behind the workers' homes and around the airplane hangar and landing strip. She'd never been in a small plane, not even during her acting career. For years, her job had been to enter the sitcom kitchen in every episode, carrying school books and talking about some kid problem. She wished she could talk to Baron about voluntarily giving up her first career for something very different. In a twisted kind of way, they had something in common.

"Why do you still want to leave?" he suddenly asked.

"I can't stay here right now," she said. She suppressed her desire to say how much she wanted to spend more time with Baron, to get to know him, to learn if she could trust him.

"Why not?"

"I—"

"Why won't you tell me? What dark secret are you hiding?"

"What makes you so sure I have a dark secret?"

"Because you're so determined not to tell me," he said.

They traveled many more yards before she spoke again. "You may be right. I am not a particularly trusting person. I have my reasons."

"What can I do to make you trust me?" he asked. He put a hand on her pommel, stopping both horses. He looked deep into her eyes.

"Who I am is all around you." He gestured at the desert land that surrounded them. "I'm a man who thinks family is important. I try to do the right thing."

"By making me a captive?"

He winced and withdrew his hand. "Sorry you feel that

way."

She waved her free hand at the buildings that represented his family duty. "I'm not part of your responsibility. How do you feel about giving up your geology career? About taking on all this?"

Baron's mouth tightened. "My kid brother almost died in service to our country. What I've been asked to do is far less."

"But you don't have a passion for ranching," she said.

"It wasn't my first choice," he acknowledged.

"Will you ever get back to geology?"

Baron stared off into the scrubby desert. "I don't know. That depends on my father and my brother."

"You had to take over because of your brother's immediate health crisis, but isn't there a plan now?"

"More like my father's emotional crisis. He's the one who abandoned the ranch. He's the one who called me up and ordered me to come home immediately."

"And you came."

"I'm the eldest son. Bad enough I'd disappointed him by not wanting to run the ranch."

She cocked her head. "Your father put a heavy guilt trip on you, didn't he?"

He said nothing.

"You should have some fellow feeling about my need to escape." She smiled, willing him to do the same.

Baron's expression didn't lighten. "Why don't you trust me with your story? I want to help," he said.

"I'm fighting my own bad past experiences."

"Men?" he asked in a rough voice.

"Yes, men have been a problem in my life."

At his frown she continued quickly. "Not how you might think."

"Tell me," he ground out.

"I don't know if I can, without revealing everything about me. I can't right now. It doesn't feel right."

"Then tell me what you can."

Their horses paced slowly along a stream shaded by a few ash trees with widespread branches. Trees in this landscape were rare.

"You're lucky to have so much water in this desert area," she said.

"Tell me why men have been a problem in your life."

She sighed. "They want things from me that I am not prepared to give."

"Most men would." He nodded. "Go on."

"I moved to Jackson Hole to reduce the number of men who pursued me."

"It worked?"

She nodded.

His eyes traveled over her, appreciating her. "Are all the men in Jackson blind?"

Addie smiled. "Busy, more like. I've been on a few dates, but the pace is much slower there."

"Slower than where?"

"Uh-uh, that would be telling," she said, wagging a finger. "Better if you don't know."

"I'll get all your secrets out of you sooner or later," Baron promised.

"I don't want you to be caught up in my mess."

"Why is your life a mess?"

"Somebody caused trouble, and I'm stuck in the middle."

"Let me help you."

She shook her head. "I can handle it. I just have to follow through on what I promised a friend." She sighed. "I shouldn't admit this but I have enjoyed not being under the same pressure here as I face in Jackson Hole. Unfortunately, I'm obligated to return, and very soon."

They rode in silence for a while.

"I'd like the chance to convince you to stay," he said, leading them to a halt in a clump of trees made by a bend in the stream. He dismounted then turned to pull her down into his arms.

"Wha—" Before she could complete her question, he was kissing her.

Addie kissed him back, putting all her yearning into the way her lips moved in response to his. Baron's arms tightened around her and crushed her softness into his hardness. His hands caressed her waist. It felt so right. Her knees felt weak.

She forced herself to pull back from his questing lips. She put her fingers over his mouth, feeling both the roughness of his beard and the softness of his lips. "No more. Please."

"Why not?" He didn't release her.

"Wrong time, wrong place. You've got guests at the house who need your attention."

"Want it, you mean."

"What's with you and your sister? Are you always so abrupt and rude with each other?"

He sighed and let his arms drop. He moved away from her. Their horses were standing exactly as they'd left them. He took the reins of his stallion and led him to the stream to drink. She led her mare as well.

As the horses drank, Addie waited in vain for Baron to answer her. Finally, she prodded him. "Aren't you going to tell me about you and Tess?"

He rubbed the back of his neck, obviously uncomfortable. "It's complicated."

"Most family issues are. Or am I making a lot out of an offhand sentence or two?" Even if she was, she wanted to know how Baron felt about his sister. He'd mentioned being hunted by pushy Paula. Yet it was Tess who'd seemed to arouse his ire when they arrived.

"My brother, JD, always was in trouble. On the ranch. At school. He was a loose cannon."

Baron leaned down and picked up a small stone, then skimmed it across the stream. It bounced twice.

"JD didn't want to go to college." He smiled a little. "All JD wanted was to join the Army and go fight in the war. Any war."

He was silent for so long she prompted him. "And?"

"My parents were against it. Tess was against it. JD's girlfriends were against it."

"Girlfriends?"

"Lots of them." He picked up another stone, but when he tossed it sideways, it sank into the water instead of skipping across. "I was for JD joining. I encouraged him. He signed up on his eighteenth birthday. Basic training went well. He went to Afghanistan. Then he went to Iraq. Then his luck ran out. An IED, a homemade bomb."

"But he's alive, right?"

"If you call it living when he's lost parts of both legs, the sight in one eye, a couple of fingers, and—" He stopped. "I can't even talk about the rest. He's a mess. He's been back for almost a year and he's still in terrible shape."

"That's why your parents now live in Cheyenne?"

"Right near the VA hospital where he is. They visit him every day."

"What about your sister?"

"Tess blames me."

"Why?"

He grimaced. "Tess says he looked up to me, his big brother. He wouldn't have joined if I'd told him not to."

"Now I get it. Sort of." Baron hadn't fully detailed the complex strands of guilt and duty in his family, but he'd said enough.

He moved toward his horse. "Let's ride again."

She walked over to where her horse grazed on the narrow ribbon of grass by the stream. The mare was well-trained and didn't object when Addie scooped up the reins and mounted.

Baron did the same. He led the way down a path that left the stream and went around a rise, toward the ridge. The horses picked their way up between cactus and tumbleweed. Other rank brush offered occasional variation in the dry, sandy terrain. A few birds flew across their path from bush to bush. Otherwise, although the air was not quiet, they saw no direct signs of life.

"What else does your sister blame on you?"

"Not backing her whim to move to Hollywood and become an actress."

Hollywood again? "Does she have acting ability?"

"Who knows? All she does is drink."

Baron led them around a hill, into another valley. He pointed at the face of a hill across a mostly dry stream bed with a trickle of water in the middle. "See that? Sandstone. They've been discovering dinosaur bones in this part of the state in formations just like it."

"Are you interested in dinosaurs?"

"I want to know what's inside rocks," he said, he eyes glued to the hill as if he yearned to wrench its secrets from it.

"After roundup is over, couldn't you take time to explore that formation?"

Baron said, "There's never time. Too damn much ranch business."

They continued along the stream around another hill, where a small cabin sat in the scrubby terrain.

"Is this what's called a line cabin?" she asked.

"Used to be, but not anymore. The property line now is way west. Let me check it first. Mice come in, and then other animals come looking for the mice," he explained.

He unholstered his shotgun from the saddle and examined the building thoroughly, then invited her inside.

She entered. "When I was a little girl, I wanted a little cottage to live in. This is nice."

"It's our hideout. From time to time, someone in the family gets fed up. Then they come out here for a day or two."

He pointed to the kitchen and toilet facilities. The small

cabin's main room was dominated by a queen-size bed.

She looked around the compact cabin, and then flung herself into a wooden rocker. "I could feel safe in a tiny place like this."

"Safe from what?"

She raised her forearms in the air, palms out. "From everything and everyone that pressures me." She sighed, relaxing.

Baron stooped next to her chair. "Tell me who pressures you."

She shrugged. "Sometimes it seems like the whole world." She shook her head. "I can't explain."

"You mean you won't," he said. "Why won't you trust me? Whatever it is, I can help you."

She stood, shaking off the moment. "Why are we here? To check for vermin?"

He rose also, and captured her hand, tugging at it, pulling her up. "To use the bed."

"Oh, no you don't," she said, resisting, but not much.

"What if I promise I won't do anything you don't want me to?" he said, flicking open her blouse snaps.

"How do you do that so—so nonchalantly? Stop it," Addie said, but she didn't bat his hands away and she let him pull her down onto the bed.

He lay there next to her for a moment, relaxing, not trying to touch her. "This feels good. You and me. A bed," he said.

"And no sex. What shall we talk about?" she asked, with a smile in her voice.

He rolled over and propped himself up on one arm,

looking down at her. "Let's talk about the sex we're going to have, sooner or later. I haven't been with anyone for a long while. I've been tested and I'm healthy. I've got condoms. What about you?"

She looked away, the heat in her face telling her she'd turned color. In a low voice she replied. "I was tested. I'm clean. I'm not on any kind of birth control."

He kissed her turned cheek lightly. "See, that wasn't so hard."

"I'm not saying I'll have sex with you," she said. Although the bed felt very comfortable and there was something equally comfortable about lying in a bed with Baron.

"You didn't say how recent it was for you," he said.

"Over two years."

"The whole time you've lived in Jackson?" His eyes echoed the incredulity in his voice.

She nodded.

"Oh, baby. No wonder you're so high strung," he said. "Come here." He made to gather her into his arms.

"We can't," she said, and sat upright. Lying down would lead her to give in.

"Sure we can." He pulled her back down, his strong arms around her. "Let me."

She looked up into his eyes then made herself look away, at the ceiling. The rough wooden of the rafters reminded her where she was. She sat up again, surprised that Baron allowed her to. "You're very persuasive, but I have a prior commitment."

"A man?"

She turned her head away. "Not in the way you mean. A

friend is depending on me."

"Is he more important to you than this?" Baron reached one hand up and boldly put it on her breast.

She shuddered with renewed desire then removed his fingers from her flesh. She couldn't quite make herself let go of his large, warm hand. "Don't ask me to choose. I met you only a few days ago."

Clearly unsatisfied by her answer, he sat up. "I won't let you go."

She eyed him in disbelief. "I am not a toy you can possess."

"I never said you were."

"You're implying that you have some right to control my actions." She put anger into her voice, to combat her strong desire to yield to him. She had to act as offended as possible, or she'd never escape the temptation Baron presented.

"That's not what I mean and you know it," he said, looking frustrated by her deliberate escalation of their argument.

"I'm still your captive." She stood up and walked out of the cabin, refastening the snaps of her western shirt as she went. She remounted her mare.

When he came out of the cabin, she said, "Take me back to Jackson Hole."

He relocked the cabin.

When he said nothing, she made a wordless sound of disgust and twitched the reins.

They rode back to the house in angry silence, but underneath her heated facade, Addie felt relief. She'd escaped the force of his desire. And hers.

# Chapter 9

Back at the ranch house compound, Addie went straight to her room after Hoot appeared and offered to groom the horses. Under the bikinis in the bureau was an old maillot that had a racer back and would allow her to swim. While not as technically revealing as the bikinis, it was so thin she was fairly sure it would be see-through once she got it wet. Let Baron look. With Tess and Paula in the house, he wouldn't be able to do more.

She found the two visitors at the pool. They'd changed into shorts and brief tops and were sitting in the shade of an umbrella table.

"I got really hot riding," she greeted them. "I hope you don't mind me taking a dip."

"No problem," Paula replied. "I recognize that suit."

"So do I," Tess looked up from the tall drink she contemplated. "I left it here because it gets invisible when wet, if you know what I mean."

"I didn't bring a suit," Addie said.

Tess waved at her. "Have at it."

"When you come out, I'm going to interrogate you," Paula said with a smile.

Addie plunged into the water. After twenty minutes of strenuous laps, her body lost its tension. She pulled up at the side of the pool.

"You're a good swimmer," Tess called. She made it sound like an accusation.

"I've been swimming since I was a little kid," Addie tossed off, careful not to mention southern California and how common backyard pools were there. Or the beach and the surfing.

She hoisted herself out and went over to a chair to get the towel she'd brought from her room.

"Are you really a horse trainer?" Tess continued. "Miss B. said you were."

Addie nodded. "Talking method."

"Most horse trainers are men," Tess said in an argumentative tone of voice.

Addie paused in wiping the water off. She leveled an inquiring glance at Tess. Tess stared back. Her chestnut eyes were the same shade as Baron's. They radiated hostility. "The horse world is changing," Addie said. She finished drying off.

"Explain," Tess demanded.

"Yes, please do tell us." Paula gestured to the other chair under the umbrella. "Sit down and have a drink. Ice tea?"

Addie accepted the offers. Paula poured a tall glass of tea from a large pitcher filled with tea, ice, and lemons. Tess's drink was clear, surely not tea.

"Go on. Explain about women horse trainers," Tess said

again.

"As horses become ornamental possessions rather than workers' tools, women get more involved with them. It's a natural progression that happens with most industries or fields."

"Huh?" Tess said.

"That's a very sophisticated way of looking at it," Paula said. "Do you have a background in psychology or behavioral economics?"

Addie shook her head. "I observe. Out here in the middle of nowhere, maybe you've mostly still got men involved with horses. Nearer the cities, where horses are a luxury item people ride for leisure, it's almost all women. Girls cleaning the stables, older girls giving riding lessons, and women owning and running the stables. Except for racing, of course."

"Our horses work," Tess exclaimed, as if Addie had somehow insulted the ranch. "This ranch is not in the middle of nowhere."

Paula said, "Yes, it is. That's why your family likes it."

Addie could like the Selkirk ranch, too, if she was here entirely of her own free will. She took a sip of her tea. Wet and cold.

"What do you do?" Addie asked Tess. Even girls from wealthy families like the Selkirks usually worked at something, or pretended to.

Tess said nothing, but Paula replied, "I'm in investment banking."

Addie followed the diversion. "How did you come to choose that field?"

"Her father's rich, and she's an only child." Tess broke in.

Paula shot her friend a quelling look. Tess drank from her glass.

Paula turned back to Addie. "When I had to learn about the family assets that would one day be mine, I became interested in finance. Which eventually, after graduate school, led to working as a fiduciary in an investment banking firm."

"Impressive." Addie considered herself well educated by Hollywood standards, but she'd stopped with a community college associate degree. She'd taken practical classes and then trained at a couple of horse farms.

"How did you get interested in horses?" Paula asked.

Addie gave her standard, severely edited back story. "I grew up near a riding stable, and rode in exchange for the usual work mucking out the stables."

"Isn't becoming a riding instructor more typical for a girl horse lover? Didn't you just say that?" Tess asked, her tone of voice challenging.

"I teach horses, instead of people," Addie replied, sticking to the facts and trying to ignore Tess's aggressive manner.

"Are you really a horse trainer?" Tess asked. Her voice slurred a bit.

Addie said, "I soothe frightened, ill-treated, or rowdy horses, and they soothe me."

"Do they really?" Paula asked, sounding surprised.

Addie turned to Paula. "I might be upset over something on a particular day, but since I know I can't allow myself to transmit those feelings to the horses, I work at putting my negative feelings aside."

"How do you do it?" Paula asked.

"Yeah, how?" Tess asked. "I could use some techniques to get rid of my negative feelings. Other than this," she said, raising her glass. She took a big gulp.

Paula gave Tess a reproachful look and turned back to Addie. "Please explain how you calm yourself before working with frightened horses."

Thankful the conversation was back on track, Addie said, "I say a mantra, a reminder. As I go to the stable to meet my first horse, I repeat it to myself."

"What do you say?" Tess asked.

Addie felt her cheeks heating a little. "The power is love."

Tess asked, "Where did you get that?"

"It's paraphrased from some eighties song my parents liked as teens."

Tess lurched onto her feet, wavering a little. She wandered her way to the edge of the pool.

"Should she be swimming in that condition?" Addie asked Paula.

"I heard that. I'm not drunk," Tess said. Her slurred words disproved her contention. She tottered around the pool's edge.

"We'll watch her," Paula replied. "I'm certified to do CPR."

"Miss Betty is a trained former nurse, too. She looked after me when I first arrived here."

"Were you ill?"

"I had a bad reaction to an allergy pill."

"I'll bet that made Baron furious. He's been hugely against drugs ever since—" Paula stopped, looking worried.

"Since Julie," Addie said. "He told me."

Paula looked relieved. "Baron's a good guy, a straight arrow. For a while, I thought I wanted to marry him. Then JD came home."

Addie didn't want to ask the obvious, but Paula answered anyway.

"I didn't switch to JD because I pity him. If anything, I pity myself because what had been a passing girl crush years ago suddenly turned into love. One-sided, at the moment." Paula laughed without humor. "I'm the one who should be drinking away my misery."

"How did you know?"

"That I love JD, not Baron? That I want the man whose body has been permanently maimed instead of his perfect older brother?"

Addie nodded. Baron's body was so perfect, so tempting.

Paula shrugged. "I went with Tess to visit JD one day. He spewed lots of bitter, nasty words. I wanted him anyway. Body destroyed, mind messed up. He's the one I want."

Paula stared into her glass. Her chin-length dark hair covered her expression.

Addie took a deep breath. "Are you and Tess roommates? You seem so close."

"She lives with her parents in Cheyenne. They visit JD every day. As soon as each visit is over, Tess looks for a drink."

"That's too bad."

"It's not a healthy situation, dragging his sister with them every time. All her parents think about is JD. They don't notice what they're doing to Tess."

"Doesn't she have a life of her own?"

"Not exactly. She doesn't have a regular job."

"Tell me about that."

"I'll do better. Tess," she called. "Come tell Addie all about your coaching business."

"Why? Does she need a life coach?" Tess's voice held a sneer, but she ambled over and threw herself down on her chair again.

"What's involved in being a life coach?" Addie asked.

"I help people focus on what they truly want in life. Retirees, kids who can't choose a college major, any age."

"You give them advice?" Addie wasn't able to hide her skepticism, given Tess's condition.

"You're wondering how could a lush like me help anybody?"

"Tess," Paula warned.

"I don't drink to excess unless I'm here, safe on the ranch," Tess said. "Back in Cheyenne, I only have enough to loosen up after those horrible visits with JD."

"I—it's not my business," Addie replied, taken aback by Tess's frankness.

"I limit myself to two or three drinks per day."

Fine words, but her elocution was mushier by the minute.

"Tell her about the life coaching," Paula said.

Tess aimed a defiant glance at her friend before pouring another drink from a second pitcher, then gulping half of it at once. "Do you really want to know?" she asked Addie.

"I've never met a life coach before."

Tess set her drink down. "When I'm not drunk, unlike

today, I give personality tests and have my clients do exercises. I help them think about what makes them happy and what stresses them. Then they commit to making changes, and I talk them through it."

"That sounds very worthwhile. Have you coached for long?"

"For a year. Ever since the move to Cheyenne."

"So things are looking up for your career?"

Tess stared at her glass. "Coaching isn't my career," she declared in a bitter tone. "It's merely the way I spend my time when we're not at the hospital. Anyway, I don't have many clients." She poured another drink and downed it all in one lengthy swallow.

Addie looked at Paula for guidance. Paula appeared pained, either by Tess's drinking or her confession.

"Baron told me you wanted to go to Los Angeles? To act?" Addie asked.

Tess snarled, "Don't talk about that. My family forced me to abandon that dream." She hurled her glass at a small piece of decorative statuary at the edge of the patio. The glass hit dead on and shattered. She sobbed once then said, "I need another drink."

Addie looked at Paula, "I didn't mean to—"

Paula shook her head a little. Addie closed her mouth. Tess grabbed another glass from the tray in the center of the table, and poured more clear liquid from the pitcher by her elbow. She took her drink and stumbled up, defying gravity, and began ambling around the pool deck again.

"Does she do this often?" Addie asked, speaking in a low

tone so Tess couldn't hear her.

"Get drunk and throw things? Whenever she can escape her parents."

"They sound like—" Addie didn't finish the thought.

"They're good people, but they don't see what they're doing to her," Paula said. "She won't drink like this tomorrow. She's just blowing off steam. Every member of this family has been adversely affected by JD's horrible injuries."

"Baron, too?" Addie asked.

Paula nodded. "When his father ran the ranch, Baron was very laid back. Now that he has the full load is on his shoulders, he's all work and no play. His women call it quits fast. That's why Tess and I were surprised to find you staying here. You're a step in the right direction."

Addie was not ready to confide the awkward truth behind her stay at the ranch. "Thanks for telling me. You've explained a lot."

Paula shrugged. "Since you're his girlfriend, you might as well understand what's eating this family."

"I'm not—"

"I went down to the stable and saw you two kissing, so don't bother denying it."

"Okay, I won't," she said, but felt her cheeks heating a little. Thank goodness she'd stopped their lovemaking. They'd thought they were completely alone. The temptation to make love right then and there had been almost overwhelming. They'd been getting into some very explicit groping, too. How embarrassing that Paula might have seen. She said she only saw them kissing, but maybe she was merely being polite about what exactly they were doing.

For the first time, Addie really looked at Paula. "You come here just to deliver Tess safely so she can grieve, don't you?"

"You could say that. I care about this family."

Baron arrived at the pool. He wore conventional baggy trunks. Addie was relieved. If he'd shown up in a Speedo, she'd likely have drooled. Even Tess would have noticed. Especially Tess, whose inebriation made her more frank than polite.

The maillot was almost dry, but still uncomfortably see-through. She didn't try to cover herself in case Baron looked her way.

Tess suddenly pointed a finger at Addie and said, "That suit is see-through. We used them when we were on the swim team. Remember, Paula?"

Baron's attention was drawn to Addie. Of course her nipples peaked. His stare grew intense.

Awkward. She was just about to pull her towel around her when Baron jumped into the water. Probably because he needed to drape a towel around himself. They were hopeless. She stifled an urge to giggle.

She'd learned some important facts about Baron's family, but she'd had enough. She said a general goodbye and went into the house. Back in her room, she showered and dressed in fresh borrowed clothes, this time a light summery dress and thong sandals she'd found in the guest room closet.

Down in the kitchen, she found Miss Betty in a frenzy of cooking, TV sitcom blasting away.

"Is there anything I can do to help?" Addie asked.

"Bless you, child. I've got it all under control." Miss Betty gave her a shrewd look. "Hoot told me you're workin' wonders with that wild stallion. You've got a talent, he says."

"Thanks. Horses are easy to understand." Addie shrugged. "Unlike men."

Miss Betty cackled. "You got that right. Men don't make a lick of sense. Never have."

Addie was about to retreat when Miss Betty stopped her labor over the bread board.

"You can set the table in the dining room if you want. Dishes in the breakfront."

In the formal dining room, Addie found sterling flatware and damask napkins as well as bone china, but nothing more casual. She stuck her head back in the kitchen. "Did you want me to use the sterling and the fancy napkins?"

"Yep. It's not every day we have so much company. Might as well use the good china, too."

Addie was arranging the tableware artistically when Baron found her. He was still in his swim trunks.

"Why'd you vanish?"

"My suit was see-through," she said.

"My big mouth. I shouldn't have ragged on you about wearing skimpy clothing." He rubbed the back of his neck. "I overreacted. I get so turned on every time I see you."

Addie's mouth dropped open.

"I need you, Addie," His arms pulled her against his bare torso. Her thin cotton dress hardly created a barrier between their flesh. She could feel every muscle in his chest. Her hands found their way to caress his nipples, even as hers hardened. Their lips entwined. He crushed her against him. His tongue delved into her mouth, and his hands caressed her hips. One hand inched up her short skirt and played with her thigh. She gasped and rubbed herself against him.

A loud bang from the kitchen brought them back to themselves.

"Addie, I want you. You want me. Why are we waiting?" he asked.

"I must return to Jackson Hole. After I do, then we'll see how we feel."

His brow darkened. "You keep saying that. I want you to stay here. With me."

She shook her head. "I won't be your captive." She turned and escaped the mingled pressure and temptation. Back in her room, she caught sight of herself. His wet body had imprinted in key spots on her dress. In addition to wet cloth over her nipples, she saw a telltale damp patch where his groin had pressed hard against her.

She groaned. She wanted him so much. He was a magnificent man. She loved his kisses. His other touches were exciting and caused her body to go hot. But how would Baron react to the vicious publicity of the tabloids? Would he think her as tainted as they pretended she was?

She changed dresses then hurried back to the dining room to finish her small task for Miss Betty. Once that was done, she wandered out to the front porch. The evening air was already cooling. There she found Paula, changed into a deceptively simple summer dress. Designer, but not obvious. "Did you want to be alone? I could go elsewhere," Addie offered.

"If I wanted to be alone, I could have stayed in Cheyenne,"

was the dry reply. "Tell me about horse…whispering, you called it? What drew you to it?"

"Kim Novak and Brigitte Bardot."

"Who?" Paula scrunched up her face, obviously trying to place the names.

"Sex symbol movie stars from mid-twentieth century. They became big animal lovers after they learned the only males to be trusted have four feet."

Paula laughed. "You must have been mighty disillusioned at an early age."

Addie took a seat on a rocker. "Nothing overly traumatic."

"How did you decide on horse whispering?"

"I visited a ranch and there was a horse who acted up for others, but was very good for me. Someone told me it was because I talked to him as if he was a puppy." She shook her head, remembering. "I must have sounded like an idiot."

"But the horse responded."

"He did, and my career was born. I'd found something I was naturally good at, something that helped the world a little bit."

"Not biochemistry or physics," Paula said, smiling.

Addie shrugged. "I wasn't university material. Helping civilize horses the right way is something I can do, and it needs to be done. We don't have to break horses. We should be humane toward the animals in our care."

"Unfortunately, we still have war, and man's vicious inhumanity to man," Paula said, obviously thinking of JD and the IED's terrible damage.

"I can't stop war," Addie said. "Peace in the stables and the corral I can manage."

"How noble. Perhaps you could widen your scope to arrange for peace in this wretched family," Tess said, sweeping out to the porch and plopping down on the glider next to Paula. Tess was also wearing a lightweight summer dress for the occasion.

Addie frowned. Was the mix of scorn and misery in Tess's voice aimed at her, or at the world in general?

Paula put an arm around Tess. "We're here to relax."

Tess shrugged off her friend's arm and leaned forward to face Addie. "Why are you at my family's ranch?"

Tess did not need to know about Addie's unplanned trip from Jackson Hole. "Baron wants me here."

"This is my home," Tess said, with a mean gleam in her eye. "I think you should leave."

"Tess." Paula voiced her disapproval in one syllable.

Addie's mouth dropped open. "Do you say that kind of thing to every woman Baron brings to the ranch?"

"And why are you wearing my clothes?" Tess asked, the anger in her expression intensifying.

Addie looked down at the simple shift and thongs she wore. "I was under the impression they were discards, available to anyone who visited."

"I don't want you wearing my clothes," Tess said.

"You're still drunk," Paula said, her voice low and sad.

"I may be drunk, but I can still tell this—this horsy girl she's not wanted here." Tess's voice rose.

"Not wanted?" Baron's deep voice repeated his sister's words, but with an angrier inflection. He stood at the door.

"Addie is a guest. Behave."

To Addie's relief, Tess subsided into sulky silence.

"Miss Betty says dinner is ready." Baron frowned. "She sent me out here to collect you all. Maybe Tess ought to skip it."

Paula nodded. She stood and urged Tess to stand, too. "Let's go to your bedroom."

"I don't feel so good," Tess said. She meekly allowed Paula to lead her into the house.

Addie stared after them.

"I apologize for my sister." Baron moved close and put his arms around Addie. "She's very unhappy and she acts up with everyone. That's why Paula brings her to the ranch."

"I feel bad. I'm wearing her clothes, living in her childhood home. Obviously, I'm in the way."

"No. I want you here." He leaned in and kissed her lips. He might have meant it to be a light kiss, but the moment their mouths touched, they took fire. His tongue and hers entwined, and their bodies strained to meld. Their arms clutched at each other restlessly.

"Dinner's ready. Where is everybody?" came Miss Betty's voice from the hall.

They broke off the embrace, each breathing deeply. They stared at each other, their eyes telling their frustrated desire.

"Dinner, I said. I cooked all afternoon." Miss Betty stood at the threshold.

Baron put his arm around Addie and pulled her close to his side. They walked into the house.

Paula joined them in the elegant dining room soon after. A little bit after that, Tess arrived. Would this be a repeat of a few minutes ago?

As dinner proceeded, Tess was on her best behavior. They spoke of innocuous things as Miss Betty insisted on bringing in heaping platters and bowls of meats, vegetables, and salads.

She refused to eat with them, saying, "I'll be listenin'. See if you children can behave yourselves for an hour. If I hear loud words, no dessert." With that, she withdrew.

Baron smoothly directed the conversation to talk of Paula's investment ideas.

"It's a great time to buy real estate, but when isn't?" she said.

"That's how the ranch got so large," Baron explained to Addie. "Our great-grandparents came out here in a covered wagon, and they held on. It was a tough life. Lots of ranches failed. As others gave up, our family bought their land and expanded our holdings."

"The rumor that we helped them fail by damming up the only water supply is false," Tess said, deadpan.

Paula laughed. "I do remember someone accusing you of that."

"Great-grandpa might have made some cutthroat deals," Baron shrugged. "He was a shrewd old guy, I hear. When a family is selling up and leaving, they'll accept whatever price is offered."

"There isn't any fortune that doesn't involve blood or tears," Paula said.

Addie nodded. Her TV earnings had cost her some tears as a child, when she'd had to work while others her age could play. Today, her accumulated fortune cost her more pain, because it made her a target of the tabloids and of men who wanted to use her.

Tess asked her brother, "Are you thinking of buying more land? Dad won't go for it."

Baron's expression soured. "Some acres on the west edge, up beyond the stream. The rock formations on that property are intriguing."

"Dad only wants land if it has additional water, to run more cattle," Tess warned.

Baron said, "I might buy that piece anyway. I saved my salary while working as a geologist."

"Be careful you don't end up land rich and cash poor," Paula cautioned.

"Speaking of that, are you poor?" Tess asked, breaking into Addie's musings.

Paula said, "Tess."

Tess persisted. "Do you have to work for a living?"

"Tess. You're out of line," Baron said.

"Stop it," Paula said.

"No, that's okay," Addie said. "I'll answer your question if you explain why you asked."

"I want to know if you're after Baron for his money," was Tess's bald reply.

Addie glanced at Baron, her abductor. The man who kept refusing to let her go home. His chagrin at the accusation was obvious. She burst out laughing. "I'm not going to enlighten you about my relationship with Baron. Although we did have some strange initial meetings," she said, giving him a sly side glance.

Baron finally cracked a smile.

Tess blinked, but like a Rottweiler with his teeth clamped on someone's leg, she refused to let go of the topic. "Are you cozying up to Baron to get at our family's assets?"

Addie thought about revealing that her accountant called her a "high net worth individual." Odds were Paula, the financial pro, knew exactly what that meant. But why should Addie play Tess's game?

Addie said. "I work because I want to do something useful with my life." She raised her glass and took a sip of water. "How about you?"

Baron said, "She means, do you buy your own booze to get so drunk?"

Tess's face turned red. "That's none of your business."

"Sure it is," Addie said, making her voice sound very reasonable. "If I was a gold-digger, I wouldn't want my rich target to have a spendthrift relative."

"How dare you call me a spendthrift?" Tess shrieked.

"Do you actually earn a living with your life coaching?"

"I—I…" Tess leapt up from the table and ran out of the room.

"No dessert for anyone," came the stern voice from the kitchen.

# Chapter 10

"I'm sure you two have things to talk about," Addie said. She rose from her chair and left the dining room.

She spent a restless evening locked in her room, wanting to avoid everyone. She was ashamed of how she'd baited Tess, who obviously was struggling with a massive drinking problem. Why Tess had settled on Addie as an enemy was a mystery, but Addie knew she should have made allowance for the alcohol.

The next morning, Paula joined Addie as she was about to take her run. Paula was wearing shorts and running shoes. "You don't mind?"

Addie shook her head. She wasn't much for talking in the morning. She talked all day to her horses.

She and Paula paced each other to the point just beyond where Baron had stopped her yesterday. Then they paused.

Paula said, "I don't like running. I make myself do it because I have a desk job."

"I run so I can maintain my patience with the horses."

Paula's mouth quirked. "Too bad you couldn't maintain it

last night with Tess."

Addie sighed. "I'm sorry about that. She was incredibly rude, but obviously very unhappy."

"Tess is stuck grieving for JD. It doesn't help."

"Does it bother you?"

Paula looked at her. "What do you think?"

Addie nodded. "Can't Tess get away from Cheyenne?"

Paula sighed. "Unfortunately, she had ambitions to be a movie star. After Julie's complete smash-up out in California, no one in the Selkirk family would hear of Tess trying her luck."

Addie nodded. "If she's drinking this much now, the frustrations of L.A. could send her around the bend."

They ran back toward the house. "I'll try to be more patient with Tess," Addie said, when she'd regained her breath a second time.

"How long are you staying?"

"That depends on Baron."

Paula gave her an inquiring look, but Addie resisted the impulse to confide. What could the other woman do to persuade Baron to let her leave? Paula was the reason Baron had wanted a "girlfriend" visiting.

Miss Betty called from the kitchen door, "Breakfast is on."

***

After Paula went upstairs to get Tess, Addie sat eating alone. As usual, the TV was on, tuned to a sitcom. Miss Betty announced that Baron would be busy this morning with the roundup. "We use the latest technology on this ranch. Got chips on all the cattle."

"Computer chips?"

"That's right," Miss Betty said, pride in her tone. "Computer microchip ear tags, they call 'em. To track the cattle and identify 'em, too. No more branding."

"The cattle still wander off?"

"No computer's gonna change animal nature."

"Are Baron and his hands rounding up all the cattle, or just the ones that went AWOL?"

"The missin' ones. The cattle wander into all kinds of spots."

"That's sounds interesting," Addie said wistfully. "I wonder if I could see some of it."

"Already arranged. After you do your horse whispering with Whitey, Hoot's gonna saddle up your mare, and you, Tess, and Paula will join Baron to look for strays. Gets you out in the fresh air."

"Sounds great." Although being around Tess might be a problem. Addie decided to finish breakfast quickly, to avoid an encounter that could sour her morning.

***

Two hours into her session with the stallion, Addie heard Hoot's call.

"I saddled you up, Miss Addie."

"All right. I'll just finish up with Whitey."

She said her usual goodbyes and rubbed the stallion's

143

sensitive neck area, then left the corral. As she mounted up, she saw Paula and Tess waiting, already on their horses. Tess had a palomino. Paula's mare was all brown.

"What is this, the all-girls cattle club?" Addie asked, smiling.

Paula grinned. Tess answered, "Out here, we learn how to handle ourselves and be useful."

Paula said, "We got a call from Baron to meet him out on the second side."

"That's what we call our south area." Tess pointed behind the ranch house.

They clicked their reins at their mounts and headed for a path Addie had not previously noticed. Past the house, it led around a small rise to a completely different vista. A large valley lay below them, with what looked like thousands of cattle grazing.

"What an amazing sight," she said.

"It's beautiful," Paula agreed.

"C'mon. Race you down." Tess took off at a gallop.

"I don't know this land. You go on," Addie said to Paula.

Paula peeled out, yelling a war whoop.

Addie followed much more sedately. The ranch had so many contrasts. Hills and streams and now this beautiful valley. The Selkirk family had enjoyed this wonderful vista for their entire lifetime.

Something in Addie's chest expanded at the thought of being so connected to a particular piece of land. She'd hoped to feel that with her property in Jackson Hole, but she hadn't. If she lived here, she'd ride out every day and look at this perfect valley and know she was in heaven.

She finally reached the bottom of the path, and caught up with Tess and Paula. Baron rode up on his stallion. He wore a cut-off t-shirt that left his arms bare and emphasized his well-developed muscles.

"I see you got the message. Follow me."

Did he mean from Miss Betty? Addie had not received any messages or been sure the ones she sent got through. She didn't like being shut off from the technology that connected her to the wider world. Was there any way she could get through to Baron? They'd gotten so close sexually, but that wasn't proof they'd let down their emotional barriers. On her part, she knew she hadn't. She dreaded the moment when Baron learned about her past. Should she tell him now? Did they know each other well enough that he would react positively? Or would he instantly reassociate her with his dead girlfriend? Julie was Baron's past, but the memory of her sad end lingered.

Anyway, he was busy right now, scarcely looking at her while he snapped out orders to his crews. The three women had their assignment to search for strays along areas where the ranch four-wheelers couldn't reach.

As she turned her horse toward their search quadrant, Addie admired how Baron looked. He was the perfect cowboy, tall in the saddle, serious looking, intensely masculine, and focused on his work. He knew how to move as one with his horse to deal with a dodging steer. She'd seen a batch of western movies when her parents were thinking of pushing her for a role in one, so she had an image in her head of what a cowboy should be. Her horse work had thrown her into company with many riders, but few looked as impressive as Baron. If she was honest, no man ever had.

Baron Selkirk. Was he the man for her? He was stubborn, wrongheaded, sure his way was the only way, and more. He was also a fantastic kisser and promised to be an amazing lover. Every woman wanted to experience sex at the level of sheer ecstasy. Baron was that lover for her, she was certain of it. Or he would be, if Addie let down her guard.

Yet she couldn't know if her attraction to him depended on the thrill of being in his power, a semi-reluctant guest on his ranch. If she had a car parked at the house, and a phone in her pocket, would she still yearn to be one with him emotionally as well as physically? Or would she merely anticipate the pleasure of sex with him, knowing she was free to walk away at any moment?

She had to be free in order to know. As long as she was his captive, even though it was obvious now that she could leave at any time, she could not make a free choice. It irked her that he was so high-handed. How dare he keep her here and try to cut off her contact with the outside world? How dare he strip all the phones off their mountings so she couldn't call her supposed drug dealer? They'd moved beyond that false idea about her, yet the phones had not returned.

He didn't see her for who she was. He kept seeing Julie and her frailties. Being desired wasn't good enough for Addie. She had to be seen and accepted as herself, her whole person. That had never happened for her, not once. All the men she'd been with—and there weren't that many—all of them had been blinded by her television acting past. They imagined she had certain actor personality stripes, and they made those up from stupid gossip about sexy starlets, not by getting to know Addie.

She wasn't an actor anymore. She'd had fun as a child actor. She'd be a liar to say it had been all work and no play. Yet when the show ended its run, she didn't cry. If only people she met as an adult could understand that part of her life was over. They didn't. They saw their image of what an actor was. She was Adrienne Jelleff, a horse whisperer who had once been a child actor. Nothing more.

\*\*\*

The roundup continued the rest of the morning. Baron and the ranch hands had long since vanished, but Tess and Paula seemed to know exactly what to do, so Addie followed their lead. They picked their way along rocky terraces to get a few more straying animals. With their part of it done, they returned to the base camp and took charge of the strays sent their way by the other ranch hands.

A few hours into their labors, they heard a car honk. Miss Betty was behind the wheel of the Jeep.

"Brought you all some lunch. Heard from Baron they've found almost all the cattle."

"That's good to know," said Addie, wiping sweat off her brow. Tess and Paula circled back to join her, and they secured their horses near a watering trough.

"Set there under those trees and eat up." Miss Betty pointed to a picnic table located in the one spot of shade.

All four women sat at the table. There wasn't much conversation at first because they were hungry. It was mostly, "Pass the salt," and, "Are there any chips?"

Finally, Tess said, "I haven't felt this useful in months."

"It's a good feeling," Addie agreed. "Baron didn't make up our task, did he?"

"So we could feel important? Nah." Tess replied.

"He'd have to assign pushing these strays to his hands if we weren't here," Paula said.

"Roundup always takes all the manpower we can muster," Tess added. "Baron used to throw himself into it, every day. He'd come back from wherever he was in the world for roundup. Since our parents moved to Cheyenne, he's been in charge of every detail. The whole shebang."

Paula said, "Being the boss has changed him for the worse."

"Why do you say that?" Addie asked.

"It's sapped all the fun out of him, for one thing," Tess said.

"He's always ordering people around," Paula replied. "Or teed off because people don't hop to obey him instantly."

"He's usually sore about somethin' these days," Miss Betty confirmed.

"And bossy, totally bossy," Tess added. "He thinks he's the boss of the whole world and everybody in it."

"You mean he was different before?" Addie asked, confused.

Paula said, "He had a laid back personality. That's why I liked to tease him. Now he's ready to get angry about everything."

Addie said, "Wow. That's huge."

Miss Betty said, "'Taint easy runnin' this place. His daddy inspired a lot of loyalty. The old timers like me sometimes don't cotton to takin' orders from a man they knew as a kid. Not when his daddy is still alive and healthy and might return anytime."

Paula asked Addie, "Does knowing this make a difference?"

"Are you and Baron serious?" Tess asked, at almost the same moment.

"I've only known him for a very short time," Addie said, sidestepping a direct answer. "Now I'm wondering if I know him at all."

"It's probably too soon, anyway," Tess said.

"I disagree," Paula said. "When it comes to love, you either know or you don't know."

"There are some complicating factors that I won't get into," Addie said. "They could affect how our relationship turns out." She shook her head. "Especially because you all say Baron has changed for the worse."

"Haven't we all?" Tess asked, her expression drooping. "I've become a drinker, and I never was before. The pressure is too much sometimes and I feel like I'm going to explode. Booze helps me cope."

"I'm sorry about last night," Addie said.

"Let's not go there," Tess said. "We were talking about my bossy, annoying, domineering brother."

"You do realize he thinks Paula comes to the ranch to pursue him?" Addie asked.

"Oh, that old thing," Paula said. "I still play up to him

every now and again, to tease him."

Addie eyed her, trying to tell if Paula meant what she said. "Are you sure?"

"Now that he's got you, doubly sure," Paula smiled. She didn't look at all upset by the idea that Baron and Addie were an item. About Tess's feelings, Addie was not so secure.

"Maybe you'll end up as my sister-in-law," Tess said.

"I hope you might consider that a good thing," Addie said, "but don't hold your breath expecting a formal announcement anytime soon."

"Are you going to live with him, and then wait around for years before hoping he'll agree to 'take it to the next level'?" Paula asked, her disapproval evident on her face. "My friends do that. It's pitiful."

"How am I supposed to know?" Addie replied. "I've never lived with a guy. Have either of you?"

"Not me. My parents and Baron wouldn't let me live with a man," Tess said.

"Nor I. My father would have bought our apartment building out from under us and evicted us rather than let me live with a boyfriend," Paula added.

Addie asked, "Do these heavy parents also expect you to still be virgins?"

Tess and Paula looked at each other and broke into sniggers.

"Oh, come on. Do they really?" Addie started laughing.

"What about your folks?" Miss Betty asked Addie.

Addie suddenly remembered there was an older person listening to their girl talk. "They assumed I was sexually active years before I even became interested in boys. They laid down a few safety rules, and that was it."

"I'd love to have parents who weren't after me all the time and wanting me to account for every minute," Tess said. "I visit the ranch because Baron ignores me as much as he can, which leaves me free."

"Why do you still live with your parents?" Addie asked.

"Whenever I talk about moving out, my mother gets this real sad look on her face, and I can't bring myself to."

"If Tess took a full-time job, or did her coaching full time, her parents would accept that she's an adult," Paula said, with the air of having delivered that piece of advice numerous times.

"They're just tryin' to make sure you're safe, since they couldn't keep JD from bein' wounded," said Miss Betty.

The reminder of JD's condition made Paula look pained. Tess's face fell. "Let's talk about something else. Have you ever been to a honky-tonk?" she asked Addie.

Baron reappeared, riding down one more group of steers. Once he had expertly pushed them into the holding pen, he dismounted and walked over to them.

"Miss Betty, have you got a cold drink for a thirsty, hard-working man?"

"Sure do," she said, leaning down to open the cooler next to her.

He picked out a beer, and popped the top. After taking a long swig, he exhaled in contentment. "That cuts the dust. Thanks."

"Are there a lot more cattle coming?" Tess asked.

He shook his head. "According to the list, no."

He turned to Addie. "We've rounded up all but a few dozen. We should be done in a couple more hours. I appreciate you all helping out."

"We're having fun," Paula said.

"Yeah, but we don't work for free," Tess said. "You have to do something for us in return."

"Like what?" he asked suspiciously.

"I don't know yet. I'll think of something," his sister replied.

"That's got me trembling in my boots. Enjoy lunch, ladies." He took off.

Addie was bemused. He had barely looked at her. Where was the focused attention she'd already come to expect from him? Should she feel piqued? Or should she feel accepted because he treated her as one of the regular ranch women who could be relied upon to help out when the sheer volume of work was too much for all his men?

Miss Betty must have noticed her staring moon-eyed after Baron. "Child, go after him. He hasn't mounted up yet."

"Not my style," Addie said, though secretly she was tempted.

Baron called out, "Addie, would you come here for a second?"

She looked at the others. They looked back at her expectantly. Miss Betty said, "Well, go on. See what the boss wants."

They each had ideas about what the boss wanted, but Addie obediently went over to where Baron was checking his horse's girth strap. She walked around his horse to the side where he stood getting ready to mount. The horse blocked the view others had of them.

"What is it?" she asked.

"Just this," he said. He seized her in his arms and kissed her.

She melted into him, feeling a sense of homecoming and belonging. When they finally came up for air, he smiled down at her.

"We should kiss more often," he said.

"You should look like a perfect dream cowboy more often," she said, pushing his hat back on his head and lightly fingering his dark hair.

He snatched another kiss.

"Gotta go, beautiful." He saddled up and turned his horse and rode away at a canter.

When she returned to the others, the women all razzed her about what she and Baron had been doing for so long behind the horse.

"What do you think we did?" she said, smiling with a hint of smugness.

"Here come more strays," Paula said, pointing down the valley. A line of cattle were being herded in their direction by a couple of ranch hands.

"I'll clean up all this," Miss Betty said. "You girls best get to work."

They all rose, and the three young women mounted up.

The roundup continued with many more cattle driven in by the ranch hands and Baron. He didn't need to do the work with them, but likely it spurred the men to make their best efforts. As for Addie, the strenuous activity was welcome despite her work with Whitey. She hated being cooped up. She couldn't ask for a bigger sky than this. The Selkirk ranch extended to the horizon in all directions.

She and Baron seemed to be moving closer. Maybe an affair, but it felt sweeter than a mere sexual thing. Maybe they had a chance together? Maybe she could even begin to fantasize that after the trial was over she and Baron might begin an honest relationship, free of misconceptions and secrets.

Was that possible? Or was he still hung up on Julie? If he knew about Addie's past, would he see her for herself, or as the epitome of evil Hollywood?

When would she get a chance to tell him about her own past? Did she even dare? Learning she'd been on a television show might get him so disgusted with her that he'd finally cave and help her get home, but they were so close now she didn't want to risk it.

\*\*\*

Baron held onto his temper with difficulty. Once again, a longtime employee, Davis, was resisting Baron's order to change a roundup tradition. The ranch hands didn't accept that he was the boss. To them, his father still was.

"Do it the way I told you to," Baron said, through gritted teeth, his ire under control but his voice showing steel. Baron stared Davis down. Davis finally nodded and turned away, walking toward the corral with reluctance in every step. Baron watched, hands clenched, wanting to shove him along faster.

Hoot Hawkins rode up on his horse, taking in the situation at a glance. "How do you want us to finish up with these stray calves, boss?" he asked.

After Baron explained briefly, Hoot nodded and joined Davis to work with the calves.

The old man's tactful manner of deferring to Baron should have soothed him. Instead, Baron's frustration increased. Davis and the others would accept what Hoot told them without argument. What would it take to get through to the crew that Baron was in charge now? He was the boss here. Why didn't anyone do what he wanted?

*** 

By late afternoon, the women had returned to the ranch house, gotten cleaned up, and were sitting around the kitchen table in casual clothes, having tea and cookies. Tess for once was not drinking anything harder. Baron hadn't returned yet.

"Turn the TV on, Miss B.," Tess said.

Miss Betty shot Addie a covert look. "Oh, I think it might be broken."

"You're a technophobe." Tess laughed. "Let me at that remote." She grabbed the device from the counter and pressed the buttons. The television turned on.

"See. No problem." She switched channels, flipping past each quickly. "Now I can hear all the Hollywood gossip."

Addie cringed inside. This wouldn't go well. Maybe she should leave the room.

With a homing instinct, Tess found a channel with a tabloid news show. Of course the announcer was avidly describing Caz's trial. Video from Jackson Hole played in the background.

"The trial of hottie television superstar Caz Cassidy has Jackson Hole all excited. Caz's trial is a spectacle like the town has never seen before."

Addie winced.

"Turn that thing off," Miss Betty said.

Tess ignored her.

Worse was to come. Close-ups of Caz, of course. Then pictures of Addie as a child actress with Caz, and lurid speculations about their relationship.

"Their love affair started when they were children on *Golden Days.* Although Adrienne Jelleff hasn't been seen in public, let alone in Hollywood, for years, Caz couldn't keep away from her."

Baron walked into the kitchen just as the television focused on blurry recent photos of Addie.

"Adrienne Jelleff's unstoppable affair with Caz Cassidy drew Leslie Tone all the way from California. Tragically, Leslie was shot at the love nest where Caz continued his sizzling affair with Adrienne. Caz is being held as the shooter, although through his legal team Caz claims he is innocent."

"Meanwhile, Leslie Tone is still hospitalized."

"And what of Adrienne Jelleff, whose wild affair with Caz Cassidy caused the shooting? The trial's outcome hinges on Adrienne Jelleff's testimony. Will she tell the whole truth about that reckless night at her secluded home?"

"Adrienne Jelleff is missing. She was spotted in Caz's hotel just a few days ago, but vanished."

The scene changed to Addie's own ranch. Her ranch manager, Trudy, unwillingly spoke to the reporters from the stable door. "She's somewhere safe. That's all I'll tell you."

The tabloid announcer continued to whip up a frenzy. "The people have a right to know the truth. Where is Adrienne Jelleff hiding? Have you seen this woman? Call or text us at—"

The photo filling the screen was blurry, but it was recognizably Addie. Everyone in the ranch kitchen turned to stare at her.

Miss Betty snatched up the remote and shut the TV. "Now see what you done," she said into the sudden silence.

"You're Adrienne Jelleff?" Tess asked.

"I guess there wouldn't be any point in denying it now," she said. She couldn't keep the bitterness out of her tone.

"A Hollywood actress," Baron said, in a voice of stone.

"A former child actor. Emphasis on former," she said.

Tess said, "No wonder you laughed when I asked if you were poor."

"I'm a horse whisperer now," Addie insisted, silently willing Baron to believe her.

"So you claim," Baron said. His face was rigid with disbelief.

Tension tightened her throat. "I'm the same person I was five minutes ago."

In the tense silence, Paula asked, "Why are you here, instead of in Jackson Hole at the trial?"

Addie stared at Baron, still not willing to reveal how he'd

held her captive. She answered without turning. "I'm avoiding the paparazzi hell."

"You were hiding from tabloid reporters when you got into my vehicle?" Baron asked.

"That's right," Addie said.

"You didn't go to the hotel for a job interview?"

"No, I went to try to calm Caz down."

"Your lover." He spat out the words.

"Friend," she emphasized. "Caz and I are friends."

"Yet when he wanted you, you came running. Despite being so sick," Baron said, his tone flat.

"He was worried about what the publicity would do to his career."

"They say there's no such thing as bad publicity," Tess said helpfully.

"Caz doesn't think so," Addie replied, not bothering to look at her.

"You know something the world doesn't?" Baron demanded. "What?"

"I'm not talking about my friendship with Caz, not even to you," Addie replied. She begged him with her eyes to accept what she said, but the steel in his expression did not soften.

"Not even me."

Baron's tight-lipped reaction was awful. She'd prefer it if he yelled.

"You lied to me," he said.

"No, I did not. I simply did not reveal all."

"You're an actress." He spat out the word.

He might as well have called her a harlot.

"It's not a crime," she said. She stood. "I can't take any more of this right now."

"Come with me," he said, in a tone that brooked no refusal. He didn't touch her. He gestured with an inclination of his head that she was to follow him out the kitchen door.

Conscious of their avid audience, she went outside with Baron. "Are you finally taking me home?" she asked, once they were in the yard.

"No," he said. His manner was icy.

"Then where are we going?" She stopped with her hands on her hips, not budging.

He picked her up and carried her to the four-wheeler by the garage. She kicked and screamed and beat on his chest. She lost her thong sandals. The other women ran out of the house and called for him to stop, but he ignored them. The usual chemistry when Baron touched her or she touched him was completely missing. He radiated hostility.

He threw her into the four-wheeler, started it, and peeled out before she had a chance to jump. He kept up a fierce speed, slewing them dangerously as he made the turn out of the yard.

"Slow down. You'll crash," she cried.

"Put your seatbelt on," Baron said in a hard voice. He drove the sport vehicle as if he was at the Indy 500, screeching around curves and thumping up and down on the unpaved road to the hills.

"Take me back to the house."

"Don't talk," he commanded. "Do as I say. I won't hurt you. You know that."

"Do I?" she asked. The tears she wanted to cry constricted her chest.

Soon they were alone in the desert, still going at a speed that would make jumping out suicide. She tried to speak to him, but he ignored her. After twenty minutes, they came to the line shack. "Oh, no. Don't you dare," she said, angry herself. Did he think she would willingly have sex with him now?

Baron stopped the vehicle, and hauled her into his arms again. Addie tried to fight him, but his right arm kept both of hers captive.

"Stop struggling," he said. He paid no attention when she tried to hit him. He carried her to the cabin and unlocked it despite her efforts to stop him. Once inside, he set her down on the wooden floor. Her bare feet registered the warmth of the desert on the planks, and their roughness.

"Do you want me to get a gun and check for vermin again?" he asked.

"You're asking me?"

"You claim you want to be away from people who bother you, that this cabin makes you feel safe. The tabloids won't find you here. You can be as alone as you want. I'll come get you in a week."

She shook her head. "I don't want to be a hermit. You can't leave me here. I don't have a phone. I don't have shoes, for god's sake."

"You don't need them. Do what I tell you. Stay here. You'll be safe."

Addie clenched her fists, resisting the urge to sock him. She said with measured accents, "I promised to help Caz."

"Let your lover be convicted."

"Caz is not my lover."

"Why should I believe you? You've refused all along to tell me anything about your life."

"So listen to me now," she said, grabbing his arm.

He shook her hand off fiercely. "You're another Hollywood addict, a fame addict. Like Julie."

"No," she cried. "I left. I'm never going back. Not tomorrow and not ten years from now. Never."

His nostrils flared and his rage was visible in his eyes. "Do what I tell you, for once, instead of arguing like everyone else."

"Don't leave me here, Baron. You have no right."

"I'm too angry to think straight," he said. "You'll be safe here."

He closed the door on her. As he locked it from the outside, she banged on the solid wood.

"Are you crazy? Let me out. Don't do this! Don't!"

His boots pounded down the steps. The four-wheeler's motor started. She screamed at the top of her lungs. She tried to open a window but it was barred and nailed shut. Even in her frenzy, she knew better than to break the glass. She'd bloody her hands.

After the sound of the vehicle dimmed, and she knew Baron was gone, she sank down on the floor, wailing. She rocked back and forth, crying. Her Hollywood past had destroyed her again. She cried for a long time.

When she was only five years old, how could she or anyone have known that playing a cute kid in a television sitcom would ruin her entire adult life? Her parents were Hollywood insiders. Negotiating the treacherous waters of the entertainment industry was their daily adventure. They sank their teeth into it and enjoyed the struggle. As a child, she'd trusted her parents to make her decisions. When the show ended, when she had to make choices herself, she learned the truth about show business.

She hated it, but she couldn't get away from it. Every time she tried to flee, it reached out and destroyed her happiness all over again.

She'd thought she had a chance with Baron. Yes, he was high-handed and domineering, but she could stick up for herself, and he'd never fully crossed the line. She was the one who hid in his SUV, after all. He'd only refused to take her back to what he imagined was a sordid drug addiction situation.

When she finally convinced him she wasn't another version of his tragic college sweetheart, she couldn't let their passion take over. She couldn't commit to him when she was still on shaky ground with him, more his captive than his guest. At any moment her past would catch up with her and change everything.

She had cherished the hope it wouldn't matter. She'd wanted to believe that Baron was the one man who would be willing to take her at face value. The one man who would see the real her, who she was today. A few minutes of sleazy tabloid television had destroyed that hope.

What did Baron think he was doing, locking her in an isolated cabin without the means to defend or protect herself?

Was he so full of rage against her, so disgusted at her that he didn't care if she got hurt? She shuddered. He wasn't that man, was he? Yet how could she know how far his anger would lead him? It was outrageous and crazy that he'd dragged her out to this cabin.

She couldn't meekly stay here for a week, and break faith with Caz. She had to escape. She couldn't let Baron's rage hurt her, and in doing so destroy him. She was damned if she'd let him hurt her.

The more power he had over her, the more danger she faced. She feared for how each of them might behave at their next encounter. Their sexual chemistry was very potent, but she could not allow him to force her to give in. Nor would she use their attraction to pay for her freedom. She had to get away on her own, and save them both.

The sun was already slanting down. She must escape this cabin while it was still daylight. The desert was too dangerous to walk at night, when she would be unable to recognize landmarks.

She examined every inch of the cabin. The kitchen drawer held a few small paring knives. Possibly they would be enough to defend herself in hand-to-hand combat with a man, assuming she knew how to fight with a knife—which she didn't. The knives were far too small to be useful fighting off a large animal or one of the many poisonous snakes in the desert. Which meant she was stuck in the cabin.

No. She refused to give up.

He'd carried her off while she was wearing a dress. No protective boots, and her thongs had fallen off back in the yard. Walking barefoot on the hot desert sand would be impossible. She didn't have a hat, either. She couldn't go anywhere, not through that rocky terrain, either in full daylight or at night.

No. She wouldn't give up.

She managed to force one window open a little, so she could hear outside noises and get some warning. She primed the pump and readied a bucket of water to douse Baron with when he returned. If that didn't cool him off, she had another surprise prepared. If it came to a serious struggle, maybe hot soup thrown at him would stop him. She would not let him hurt her. She stifled a sob at the thought that he might. Perhaps her imagination was working overtime. He had never physically harmed her. Nor had he threatened her. But remaining a prisoner in this cabin was intolerable.

When she searched the cabin more thoroughly, she discovered a locked box on a top shelf. She used one of the precious knives to jimmy the lock. The blade broke, and she started crying again. She wiped her tears away with a dish towel and turned the blade with the cloth. Finally, the lock yielded.

Inside the box she found a treasure trove. Strong, thin rope. Matches. A Swiss army knife. Real survival gear.

Except she was barefoot.

She began the arduous task of cutting up blankets and using the rope to fashion makeshift footwear.

Too many minutes later, she had turned the blankets into moccasins stiffened with cardboard from cartons in the pantry and threaded with rope to keep them on her feet. She'd made a rope belt to hang her tools on, and a crude backpack with bottles she'd filled with water. The remainder of the blanket she'd hacked into a rough kerchief to keep the sun off her head, although it was getting late and the sun was low in the sky. She was ready to escape.

Now all she had to do was break out of the cabin.

A noise came from outside. She started the soup on the stove, in case she didn't have time to escape after all. Then she went to work on the window.

The noise didn't recur. She kept working. In the end, it was easy. She used a hammer and a screwdriver together to chisel out the window completely, including the frame. The bars were attached to the frame, so they went, too.

She set the window on the floor and put the last of the blanket on the exposed wall, covering the rough spots. She grabbed her makeshift backpack, checked the ground outside for snakes, and tossed it out. She followed, carefully grasping the cabin's frame until she could jump the last few feet.

She hit the ground. Free. The sun hadn't set, but there wasn't much time to orient herself and hike to the crew's compound. She tried to remember the exact path they'd taken only a few hours ago. The cabin was set behind a hill. She began to walk around it.

No one had stopped Baron. His womenfolk were too intimidated. Were they all too shocked? Including herself? She hadn't fought hard enough. She'd let him take her to that prison cell. What a fool she'd been.

It was nearly over. The crew of ranch hands included men who had the backbone to challenge Baron over ranch procedures. Surely one of them would dare to help her. Maybe Hoot would. All she needed was one person with a vehicle, and she could leave the ranch.

Despite the sun's low position in the sky, her feet quickly burned through her cardboard sandals. The sandy soil radiated the day's heat. Up top she was more comfortable, as the sleeveless shift she wore kept the rest of her well ventilated. If her trek took long, she'd start shivering as the desert cooled in the evening.

The shift had no pockets. Her wallet was back in her bedroom and, with it, her cash. One foot in front of the other. She'd deal with her lack of travel funds once she got back to civilization.

A familiar noise stopped her. A Jeep crested the ridge and bore down on her.

There was nowhere to hide. The bushes were low scrub, too small to duck behind. She pulled her knife from her makeshift belt. She would not allow Baron to take her back to that prison.

The Jeep drew closer and slowed down. Tess was at the wheel. She screeched the vehicle to a stop and jumped out.

"Are you okay?" Tess hugged her. She drew back and examined Addie. "Oh, my god. He even took your shoes."

"No, the stupid thongs fell off."

"You're giving my brother too much credit," Tess said. Her tightly pursed lips and the hardness in her eyes radiated her anger. "Running this ranch has done something to Baron's head."

"You got that right." Addie sighed. "How did you know I

was here?"

"Hoot followed you. Took Whitey. If you hadn't calmed that horse down, Hoot couldn't have ridden him despite all his years of rodeoing. He told me he didn't have time to go to the ranch hands' stables for a fresh horse."

They climbed into the Jeep and Tess started it up. The vast distance back to human habitation was reduced to nothing. Sunset was no threat now.

"We were all worried when Baron came back alone. He looked like he had done murder."

Addie shuddered. "Let's not go there."

"Hoot came to the house and told us what he saw. Then Miss Betty finally admitted the truth about Baron bringing you to the ranch against your will and refusing to let you leave. No wonder you were wearing my clothes."

"I thought I could convince him to let me go. Up until that nasty tabloid show."

"Was even half of what it claimed true?"

"Not the part about me and Caz. Who cares about the rest?"

"Baron."

Addie sighed. "Hollywood strikes again. Another potential relationship gone to hell. I don't want to go back to the house. I don't want to see him again for a while. Maybe never."

Tess let out a dry laugh. "No worries," she said, "Baron is rip-roaring drunk at the moment and incapable of any action. I spiked his lemonade with vodka. Miss Betty and Paula locked him in his office. For good measure, we took his boots."

"Poetic justice." Addie said. She sighed. "I've been a fool, hoping we could build something despite his preconceived notions and my evasions. Now I need to go home."

"I'll help."

"Can you?"

"Darn right I can." Tess maneuvered the Jeep over the ridge to the ranch hands' compound, then past it. "Paula flew the plane that brought us here. I'm taking you straight to the air strip. She's getting ready to fly you out."

"That's fantastic. I owe you one."

Tess shot her a dark look. "You don't. Our family mess is to blame. Baron never acted like this before. Ever."

"Maybe it's the sexual frustration," Addie said. "Men always claim it drives them nuts. Maybe it really does."

Tess glanced at her. "You mean you never did it? Not even once? I saw the way you looked at each other."

Addie shook her head. "As long as I was a prisoner here, I would never have made love with Baron. Not voluntarily, anyway." She shuddered.

"Did you think he might—?"

"I don't know. That would have ruined us both."

Tess cursed Baron and all men. "Tell me about Hollywood. I've always dreamed of going there, yet you left."

"It was okay when I was a kid, but as an adult, I had it tougher."

"The fabled casting couch? Grabby producers wanting sex in exchange for a role?"

Addie nodded. "Avoiding them took some fast talking—and a few threats."

Tess cursed again.

"Of course, Baron probably thinks my life in California was all sequins and klieg lights."

"And sex with Chris Hemsworth."

"They never look like Chris Hemsworth." She choked back a laugh. "That's the problem."

Tess guffawed.

The laughter made something in Addie's chest relax. "Thanks for helping me find the humor in this. For the last few hours I've been in dire straits," she said.

"Tess and Paula to the rescue. She'll radio for clearance from the Jackson Hole airport. Why don't you use my cell phone and call someone to meet you there?"

Addie called her manager, Trudy, and then Caz's lawyer, Marty Feld. He was freaked out.

"Thank god you called. The trial's going faster than we expected. We need you to testify tomorrow morning. We tried to delay, since no one could get hold of you. Trudy gave us the number, but we never got through to a live person, just a recording."

"I hope this is a secure line," she said. "Tabloids have been known to hack people's phones."

"I'm an officer of the court. That makes hacking me a bigger crime."

Marty promised to arrange for someone to meet her at the private plane section of the airport, to which the paparazzi did not have access.

Tess was as good as her word. She screeched the Jeep to a halt in front of the hangar.

Paula came out from behind the small plane. "You okay,

Addie? He didn't hurt you?"

"I'm good. Getting better every minute."

Paula handed Addie an athletic bag. "From Miss Betty."

"Oh, wonderful. My clothes. My boots." She caressed the boots. "My wallet, too. Thank you." She went inside the hangar and wasted no time changing into her jeans and putting on real footgear. In a minute she was ready.

Paula motioned her to the plane. "I'm positioned for takeoff. Let's go."

Addie went over to hug Tess. "Thank you. I won't forget this."

"When Baron kicks me off the ranch, I'll try to remember that," Tess said. She grinned. "I love putting one over on my big brother."

Paula and Addie boarded the small aircraft and buckled into their seats.

"What will happen to you when he realizes you got me out?" Addie asked.

"Baron can ban me from the ranch, but not from seeing JD." Paula donned a headset and handed one to Addie, then started her preflight check of all the instruments.

Addie shivered from reaction. She was finally escaping. Hard to believe. She'd never thought a plane would be an option.

Paula started the takeoff. They waved through the windows to Tess as they taxied down the runway. Within a few seconds, they were airborne. "We should make Jackson Hole by sunset."

Addie sighed with relief.

After a few minutes, they settled into a flight path and Paula turned on the automatic pilot. "If you don't mind my asking, why did Baron lock you in that cabin?"

"He said he was keeping me safe from the tabloids."

"That doesn't make sense."

"How did I get so mixed up with his past? Am I anything like Baron's dead girlfriend?"

Paula shook her head. "Julie was a wimpy thing. Easy for Baron to feel protective about."

"That's not me," Addie said.

"No, not from the little I've seen of you. Anyway, following him around the world, or worse, staying home alone while his geology career took him away constantly, was not for her. She wanted bright lights and the adulation of crowds."

"She had the typical false image of Hollywood fame," Addie said.

"She wanted a different life, even though it killed her. You're not like her at all."

"I would love to live in the middle of nowhere and never see a stranger's face for weeks or months at a time," Addie said. "My ranch in Jackson Hole wasn't isolated enough."

"You'd be perfect for Baron."

"If he ever gets over his mad."

"'Gets over his mad' is putting it lightly, don't you think?" Paula said, with a sober expression on her face.

Addie watched the desert scrub below change to pine trees. "Earlier today, you said Baron had changed, that he wasn't like this before."

"It started last year. Geology isn't a career that gives a man

171

people management skills, as far as I know. Yet Baron was forced overnight to take the reins here."

"With no help from his parents?"

"They've completely checked out. They're no help to anyone, if you want the truth. Hoot let on that Baron's been having a tough time getting the ranch hands to accept him as the boss."

"Yes, Baron told me. Maybe that's why he kept trying to boss me. He couldn't turn it off," Addie said, and lapsed into silence.

As Paula kept watch on the flight's progress, Addie idly considered taking flying lessons. If she intended to live in an isolated area, she should know how to fly a plane. What other survival skills did she need out here? The ability to get through to a pigheaded man when he was fit to be tied, for one. Because she would never let Baron, or any other man, make her a captive again. Even when the captivity was meant to help her and keep her safe.

Did it have to be another man? She thought she'd finally found the right man in Baron. Too sure his way was the only way, but basically a good man.

Her thoughts went around and around as Paula flew the short hop to Jackson Hole. The trip that took hours by car was a mere few minutes in the plane. The sun had just gone behind the mountains when Paula landed the small aircraft at the Jackson Hole airport.

Paula taxied to the side reserved for small planes. She did her final instrument check as Addie leapt out. Her boots struck the tarmac, solid as her makeshift mocs hadn't been. No more rope belt, either.

A limo driver approached Addie and spoke a code word. After locking the plane, Paula joined them.

"Where can we take you?" Addie asked her.

"Just drop me at a local motel."

"What will you do next?"

"I'm going back to Cheyenne. Back to JD."

They drove through the gathering evening gloom silently once Paula had called and found an available motel room. The limo drew up just outside the perimeter of light at the chain motel.

"I apologize for not getting you closer," Addie said, "but we have to keep me a low profile."

"I understand."

"JD's an idiot if he doesn't recognize what a rock you are," Addie said, touching Paula's arm. "I can't thank you enough. You're a heroine."

Paula smiled crookedly. "I hope that's enough to sustain me while I wait JD out."

Addie nodded. "We'll meet again."

"We will," Paula promised.

They hugged briefly. Paula exited the limo and walked across to the glass doors of the motel office.

Tears trickled down Addie's face. She'd found a stalwart friend in Paula. Tess, too.

# Chapter 11

Addie's limo pulled into the same hotel garage where it all started. Caz's lawyer, Marty, tossed in a housemaid's uniform and waited outside the tinted windows while she changed. Once she donned it, with the accompanying dark-haired wig, she looked the part. They walked to the hotel door, where Marty gave her a couple of pillows to hold. She became invisible. People didn't look at maids' faces, just at what they carried.

He used a key that allowed them to take the service elevator. On a guest floor, they walked down a hall until Marty consulted a check-in folder and stopped before a door. He inserted the key to a compact room. "I had my assistant gather some clothes for you from your place," he said, as Addie checked it out.

"Thanks."

Promising to be back in the morning with breakfast, he sketched a salute, handed her the key card, and left.

Addie contemplated the simple key card in her hand. If only Baron hadn't tried to keep her a prisoner. She burst into tears.

The adrenaline that had sustained her since her rescue from the cabin dropped away. She could barely put one foot ahead of another. She leaned against the entrance wall and covered her mouth so whoever was in the next room couldn't hear her wailing.

Eventually, the worst of the storm passed. She dragged herself to the bathroom and threw off her clothes. After turning the shower on, she stood under the water and held the grab bar so she couldn't fall. She washed the dirt and dust of the cabin off her, ruthlessly scrubbing her damaged hands that only a few hours ago had desperately held a bare knife blade.

A fresh gust of tears hit her, mingling with the hot water. She'd been so desperate she'd made plans to try to save her life in case Baron came back intent on harming her. How could their relationship reach such a point of wretchedness that she feared he intended violence against her? Had they been doomed from the moment he wouldn't drive her back to Jackson Hole? All the rocky scenes between them had culminated in him treating her like a criminal merely because she'd once been on television, and physically imprisoning her in a remote and dangerous spot, without any means of contacting anyone for help. Did one act of outrageous domination lead to another and another and another? To prevent his downward spiral of behavior that led to savagery, should she have thrown herself out of the SUV that first day—no matter how fast he'd been driving?

No, none of this was her fault. She'd been ill and hunted when she hid in his vehicle. She hadn't been thinking straight, perhaps, but she'd meant no harm. The bad reaction to the allergy pill had made her weak and knocked her out. Everything that happened after she fell asleep was the direct result of Baron's insistence on being the boss.

Why did he believe he had a right to lock her up? Baron had the benefit of a sound family upbringing, plenty of material goods, and extensive education. Yet he'd behaved one step next to a cave man.

Tess and Paula had saved them both from discovering how savage Baron could become. She shivered and turned the water hotter. Perhaps his angry determination to control her stemmed, as Paula had argued, from the frustrations involved in running the ranch. In a man's world, being openly disobeyed by employees would be hard to take. Whether that was the situation or not, Baron needed to learn a different way to handle his frustration.

She turned off the water, determined to get some sleep despite the questions that went around and around in her head.

***

The next day, Addie dressed carefully and wore the full makeup Marty's assistant had provided, knowing her face would be photographed extensively. A sober royal blue dress, black pumps, and a simple gold chain as her only jewelry made up her costume. She looked the part of the best friend.

Baron might think her role was the repentant whore. No, she had to stop thinking about what negative opinions Baron might have about her. They were wrong, for one thing. He had no right, for another.

Caz fell on her neck when she joined him in a private room at the courthouse. "You got here. I was so worried."

She patted his back. "Me, too. It took two heroines to rescue me from the hero who rescued me from the paparazzi."

"Huh?" He wrinkled his forehead.

"Later. Let's get you exonerated."

Within minutes, they were called to the courtroom. They were careful not to touch each other as they walked side by side, with Caz's legal team running interference as they passed the scrum of reporters shouting at them.

"Adrienne. Honey. Turn this way. Pose for me, baby."

"Adsy, kiss Caz for us. You know you love him."

"Caz, how does it feel to have your lover finally by your side?"

Addie resisted rolling her eyes at the silly efforts by the press to break her silence, or Caz's. He'd donned a poker face, his "I'm a serious cop" look from his TV series. His walk had some of the swagger of the character he played, as well. She kept her expression neutral, trying not to broadcast any personality at all.

The gauntlet they walked seemed endless, but most of the reporters were barred from entering the courtroom. She and Caz sat where his lawyers directed, he at the defendant's table, she slightly behind him in the first row.

Addie blanked out the next minutes, but roused when she was called to the stand. After being sworn in, and having a microphone attached, she sat down and waited for the D.A.'s questions, all of which she expected to be insinuating and nasty.

He didn't disappoint her.

\*\*\*

Baron woke on the floor of his office with the light of dawn. Stiff and achy, he felt hung over. What the hell had been in that lemonade Tess gave him? It had hit him like a ton of bricks. He was a cheap drunk, which was why he didn't drink.

He threw some cold water on his face in the hall bathroom. Addie. He'd left her in the cabin all night. He hadn't meant to. Better not think about his intentions last night. None of them had been good. He'd been angry. He was always angry since coming back to the ranch.

He took off outside, pausing in the dawn. The Jeep was missing from its usual spot. No time to waste saddling a horse. He grabbed one of the lighter vehicles, a four-wheeler, and aimed for the cabin.

The smell of smoke was his first inkling. He maneuvered the four-wheeler around some rocks and a bend in the terrain, and suddenly the smoking ruin of what had been the cabin was before him.

"No!" His howl went up to the heavens. "No, no, no!"

He tore off of the vehicle and threw himself at the embers of what had been the cabin.

Addie. Oh, my god. Oh, my god.

His hoarse pleas rent the air. "Addie. Addie. Answer me. Please."

He burned his hands, but paid no mind. The fire must have started on the stove, which remained, scorched metal, akilter on the ground after it had burned through the floor and set the floorboards and everything in the cabin ablaze. The bedstead, also metal, was visible under the collapsed sheet metal roof. The metal was still hot. It singed his fingers. He ignored the pain.

"Addie. Addie."

Nothing could have lived through the inferno that destroyed the cabin so completely.

No one could have lived. Addie. Addie.

\*\*\*

He'd shoved all the roof pieces aside. He hadn't found Addie. He spent the next minutes frantically searching every piece that remained of the cabin all over again. Then under and behind every stick and bush immediately nearby. Only sheer luck had kept the cabin from starting a brush fire.

Addie. Where was her body?

Sheer luck.

Finally, his head cleared a little. He noticed Jeep tracks. He'd been raised to notice tracks. He should have noticed that a Jeep had been there.

On automatic, he remounted the four-wheeler and followed the tracks. His hands stung but he ignored them. The tracks led to the airstrip.

Had Addie escaped? Had someone rescued her before the fire turned the cabin into a smoking ruin? He prayed.

***

Tess found Baron hours later, sitting at his favorite thinking spot, a huge rock that overlooked their sprawling ranch land. He held his pistol between his knees.

He roused himself. "Tell me she's safe."

"Paula flew her to Jackson Hole last night."

He bowed his head, and told her about the cabin. "If she'd died because of my arrogant stupidity, I would have eaten this." He indicated his gun.

"Put your damn gun away," Tess said. "Hasn't our family suffered enough from violence?"

He shoved his gun in the belt in the small of his back. "We're a fine couple of losers, aren't we?"

She sat next to him on the rock, pushing him over with her hip. "I'll stop drinking if you stop acting as if your every word is law."

He laughed, but there was no humor in the sound. "I don't even know where to start."

"Start by apologizing."

"She'll never forgive me."

Tess shrugged. "She might not. You still have another fifty or sixty years to live. You can keep trying. Or there will be other women."

"There's no one like Addie," he said. "She's so amazing. She's smart, and she's beautiful, and she's kind. You should see her coo at the horses. It's as if she's full of love and there's always plenty to share."

"You wanted that."

"I knew from the moment I first saw her that she was mine."

"You did a lousy job convincing her." Tess shook her head, clearly disgusted with him.

"I wasted a lot of time accusing her of being a drug addict like Julie."

"You're an idiot. She's nothing like Julie," Tess said.

"Addie was right to leave me. I came too close to doing her violence."

She swatted his shoulder. "Did you hit her?"

"No."

"Did you...rape her?"

"No, of course not," he said, indignation in his voice.

"Were you planning to starve her into submission?"

"No."

"Will you ever lock her up anywhere ever again?"

He raised tortured eyes to his little sister, his sister whose own pain-filled eyes saw his wretchedness and somehow forgave his folly. "I thought she burned to death."

He lowered his head. He covered his eyes with his hand, and his shoulders shook. "I almost murdered the woman I love." The agonized words were wrenched from him.

Tess hugged him.

Minutes went by. Finally, he took a deep breath. "I was an arrogant fool. My opinions, my needs were more important than anyone else's. I couldn't see the truth in her."

"My brother the tyrant," she said.

"Don't make light of what I did."

"I'm not. If someday she lets you crawl to her and

apologize, you'll be lucky." She stood. "Don't expect more. She can find another man anytime she wants."

"I don't deserve her, but no one will ever love her like I do."

"Fine, but you'll have to love her from afar right now. She's busy testifying in court."

"Today?" He looked up, a surprised expression on his face.

"She's been on TV all morning. I recorded the whole session. She looks fantastic."

He straightened. "I want to see her. I need to see her."

He stood, but she put a hand out. "Wait. First, let's talk about how you and I are going to fix our family situation, so I can stop drinking and you won't act like a Neanderthal anymore."

# Chapter 12

The D.A. had the floor all morning, and his political hopes were obvious to everyone in the room. His case against Caz was ridiculously weak. A couple of times Addie had to remind the D.A. that Leslie broke into her house.

"You say you didn't invite Leslie Tone," the D.A. purred.

"That's right. I did not."

"Then how was he shot in your so-called great room?" Somehow, the D.A. managed to put a sneer into his question.

"He broke into my house through a bedroom window. Then he confronted Caz and me in the living room. Then he shot himself."

"So you say," the D.A. sniffed.

Addie turned to the judge. "Your honor, I have testified under oath. My home was broken into by a total stranger who shot himself in my presence, after threatening to shoot me and my friend."

The judge slanted a stern look at the D.A. "What's your justification?"

"Your honor, I am trying to show that the witness is not

telling the whole truth about her relationship with the defendant and with Leslie Tone."

Marty shot up from his seat. "Your honor, I object."

"Objection sustained. Confine yourself to asking about facts, not making lurid speculations."

The D.A. kept trying. Every other sentence out of his mouth was a suggestive comment about her supposedly exciting love life with Caz.

Caz's attorney jumped up and objected every time. "You honor, Miss Jelleff is both the victim of a crime and a witness to a crime. She's not a defendant. I object to counsel's attempts to impugn her morals and behavior. His whole line of questioning is incompetent, irrelevant, and immaterial."

"Now where have I heard that phrase before?" the judge asked, sarcasm in every word. "Sustained, Perry Mason."

Despite his best efforts, the D.A. could not get Addie to budge from her story that Leslie Tone was a stranger.

"Yet Leslie Tone called the defendant and you by name. He claims he knows you," the D.A. said, in an insinuating tone of voice.

Addie didn't allow herself to smile when she gave her answer. "He might have seen me as a child on a television show that millions of people watched. Recognizing my name from that show, or even my likeness, does not prove he knows me personally."

"Yet his car contained numerous photos of you."

"Many publicity photos of me from my acting days exist."

"Your honor," Caz's attorney objected. "Counsel keeps asking the same question. The witness has answered. May we move on?"

"Objection sustained." The judge directed the D.A. to stop dancing around the same question.

The D.A. was determined to play to the media circus. He moved on to questions that presumed her nonexistent affair with Caz. The insinuations got nastier as the day wore on. Addie was still on the stand when they broke for lunch.

Marty quickly went to her and unclipped her microphone. "You're doing fine. Let's get you some lunch to keep up your strength."

"I'm wrung out. Five minutes of testimony is turning into a whole day." She kept her poker face although she wanted to shoot the D.A. a dirty look.

"Maintain your calm demeanor, and we'll get through this. You're helping Caz tremendously."

"Nice of you to say so."

"Remember not to say anything outside this room, where you might be recorded by the scum that calls itself reporters." When they reached the courtroom door, Marty said, "Don't smile, but don't frown, either."

She raised an eyebrow. "You're expecting a lot. I hope it's a good lunch."

"The best Jackson Hole has to offer," he promised.

The courtroom door opened and they hit a wall of excited reporters, all shouting at her at once. Addie mentally recited her horse whispering mantra, "The power is love." She and the attorney moved steadily through the crowd with the help of the local police. Finally, they gained the sanctuary of a private room again.

"That was worse than horrible," she exclaimed. "I hate those cannibals who call themselves journalists. My next home will be in Antarctica."

Caz was in the room, pacing instead of eating. His obvious distress pulled Addie out of her own. She checked out the table laden with sandwiches and salads, and picked up a plate.

"Caz, come and eat."

Caz sat down, and took a sandwich. "When will they get to me?"

"Tomorrow or the next day," the lawyer said.

"At the rate the D.A.'s going, it'll be next week," Addie said. "He repeats every question at least five different ways."

"You've answered them all the same, which is great. You're doing fine," said Marty.

"Just think," she said. "I could have stayed on the ranch as a prisoner of a man who despises actors."

That got Caz's attention. "What was up with that? Your ranch manager said you were with some guy."

"Met him at your hotel. I was swept off my feet. He carried me to his ranch. Wouldn't take no for an answer." She made sure Caz saw the twinkle in her eyes as she finished her fanciful version of three emotional days. "He even introduced me to his sister." She wiggled her eyebrows, as they both used to do when they were kids.

Caz burst into laughter. The lawyer sent her a grateful look. Addie forgot her own woes and spent the rest of lunch teasing Caz.

\*\*\*

The afternoon in court was more of the same nastily phrased questions insinuating a lurid relationship between Addie and Caz. Also between Addie and the stalker, despite her repeated insistence that she'd never met him before he broke into her house.

As she answered the same questions over and over, steadily and without looking annoyed, she thought about Baron's stubborn way of leaping to unfounded conclusions about her and refusing to let them go. She'd been free to debate and argue with him, and sometimes it appeared she convinced him, but he always returned to his original conclusions about her. He wanted to believe she was weak, and he should make decisions on her behalf. The D.A. wanted to believe she was a Hollywood party girl despite a complete lack of evidence.

Addie began to enjoy herself a little. She was a better trained actor than the D.A. She could repeat herself endlessly without getting worked up. She had the advantage over him, because she'd done take after take of the same lines of dialogue, day after day, week after week, year after year. She was a veteran of repetition.

Finally, she wore him out. He couldn't get a rise out of her, and she didn't change her story. The jurors were bored. Even the judge was nodding off.

"I'm through with this witness," the D.A. said.

The judge promptly banged his gavel and woke up the jurors. "Court is adjourned until tomorrow morning."

As the court sergeant-at-arms repeated the judge's order, Addie stood up on rubbery legs. She'd been sitting for hours. Marty came over to her again to help her. After her microphone was unclipped, he whispered, "The jurors really like you. You've won them over by being a lady in the face of so many sleazy insinuations."

"I hope that will help Caz."

"I'm sure of it."

The legal team led her and Caz out of the building, making no public comments other than, "My client will soon be exonerated" to the encampment of photographers and reporters on the courthouse steps. The lawyers helped Caz and Addie into a waiting limo and they took off. Of course some reporters followed them, but the limo had special permission to enter the hotel garage directly, while other cars were kept back. They were met by the hotel manager and spirited up to Caz's suite via the service elevator.

Once they were in Caz's suite, Addie said, "I'd like to go to my room and rest now."

"We've moved you into the second bedroom here, where you'll be more protected," Marty said. "Last night we could put you in a regular guest room because we had the element of surprise."

She nodded. "Okay." She moved to the hall. "Which room is mine?"

Caz showed her into a large, luxurious room decorated in cozy ski lodge style. He gave her a hug. "Thank you. Thank you so much for what you're doing."

"Anytime."

After a reviving shower, Addie prowled her bedroom. She was a prisoner again. She couldn't go anywhere. Her life was on hold. She could go out to the living room and listen to the lawyers strategizing, but she'd had enough for one day. Tomorrow morning they could feed her her lines so Caz's team could make the most of her cross-examination.

She lay down on the chaise positioned by a window and looked out at the beautiful scenery. The tall fir trees were a deep green, refreshing even in summer. In the winter, their color kept the landscape from looking barren and lifeless. She loved the drama of the mountains, the way they contrasted with the azure blue skies so typical here. Some of the mountains were snow-capped year round. What a beautiful place to live. A shame she'd have to sell up and leave. After this mockery of a trial, she'd never be left alone. From now on, she'd be a hunted local celebrity. Her past would define her future all over again.

She'd found respite in Jackson Hole for two years, but no more. For a day or two, she'd hoped she could find renewed peace with Baron Selkirk. Had she fallen in love with him? She feared she had, but whatever demons possessed him were beyond her vanquishing. He had to let go of Julie and her sad story. He had to look at Addie with trust in his heart. He had to stop trying to control her.

Desire was so simple. Go with the impulses brought on by pheromones and opportunity. How easy it was to find sex, to enjoy sex. How empty. Love was so much more complicated. She preferred to save her affection for horses. They never lied. They never betrayed. Even the ones who'd been hurt, who distrusted people, could be brought around. She earned their trust by being consistent. They never turned on her. Horses distinguished between the humans who treated them badly and the ones who were kind to them. Why couldn't Baron recognize that she was not his dead love, Julie? Perhaps it was ego on her part to have thought she could gentle Baron and earn his trust. That wretched scene at the cabin was proof she'd failed.

He was so handsome, so sexy, so appealing. Every kiss, every touch had set her afire. Why couldn't it have worked out? He'd seemed a decent man, a well-grounded man. But when he looked at her, he kept seeing another woman. He assumed Addie had the same personality traits and weak habits that had belonged to his lost Julie, so he wanted to boss Addie for her own good.

Tess and Paula both said the bossiness was new. Before JD's tragedy, before being forced to give up a career in geology to run the ranch, Baron supposedly had not been so absolutely determined to be obeyed. His history with Julie showed the truth of that, since he'd let her make her own choice to stay in Hollywood. If he'd been super bossy back then, he would have dragged her back home from that California den of iniquity and locked her in the cabin. But he hadn't.

Addie was at fault, too. She hadn't been honest about who she was. How could he see Addie clearly if she didn't tell him the truth about herself? She'd demanded his trust but she had never trusted him.

Still, Baron's reaction went over the top. He took her past as a personal affront, a personal betrayal. He'd accused her of lying to him. She had, by omission. Yet after hearing about Julie's sad life in Hollywood, how could Addie casually say, "By the way, I was a child actor for seven years in a popular sitcom. You may have heard of me."

She had never found the right moment for the revelation Baron would not want to hear. She'd been right to fear his reaction. When he was forced to learn about her past, he was outraged. Why outrage? Because in his domain, he was supposed to be the boss? Because what he imagined her past had been did not suit his idea of what his life should be? Or was it something darker, something to do with his desire to fully own his woman, to control her completely because she had no other life than through him?

She shuddered. As attractive as a night of sex with a dominating man was, the thought of living with such a man turned her off. She didn't want or need to live her life by someone else's rules. She didn't want a man to break her and own her. She wanted to give herself freely. She wanted a woman whisperer. Did such a man even exist?

*   *   *

Addie and Caz spent the evening playing board games and watching a silly movie. They obeyed Marty's injunction not to check out any trial reportage. He or his assistants came and went, providing food and clothing for the next day in court. To her surprise, she slept well that night, without tears.

*   *   *

The second day of her testimony, Addie wore another lawyer-picked dress, this time a rich maroon color that complemented her light blonde hair. Under Marty's skillful questioning, she spoke affectionately about her easy friendship with Caz.

"Sometimes we go bowling. Or we take in a movie in an actual theater. Simple stuff."

"Why did the defendant come to Jackson Hole?"

"I'd been living here for two years, loving it, and I wanted him to see the new life I'd made here."

"Was there any romantic element to his visit?"

"No. We're just friends with a shared childhood. Romance between us would feel icky."

The courtroom erupted in laughter. The judge banged his gavel. "Order."

The attorney continued his questioning. "Why aren't you romantically involved with Caz Cassidy? He's been called the sexiest man alive by celebrity magazines."

"He was my TV brother for so long I still think of him as a brother." Out of the corner of her eye, she could see jurors nodding.

"Lead us through the events of the night of the crime."

Addie described the man suddenly appearing in her house, claiming he loved Caz.

The D.A. objected, "This wasn't covered in direct examination of this witness, your honor."

The judge sourly responded, "You could have asked these questions, but you wasted the court's time with your repeated questions about the witness's relationship with the defendant. Overruled."

Marty continued. "When you saw the intruder, who did you think he was?"

"A star stalker," she said.

Muttering broke out in the courtroom. The judge banged his gavel. "Order."

"What happened next?"

"Caz said, 'I told you not to keep following me everywhere'."

"How can you remember his exact words?" Marty asked.

"I learned how to memorize dialogue when I was a child actor." Her statement caused a murmur in the courtroom.

"What happened next?"

"The intruder pulled out a gun." She paused, remembering the horrible scene.

The lawyer prompted her again. "And then?"

"He waved the gun around. Then he said, 'I'll show you how much I care'." She swallowed.

"Go on, please."

"I'm sorry. This is difficult. The intruder pointed the gun at me, and then at himself. Then he shot himself." She covered her face with her hands.

"I'm sorry this is upsetting, but the court needs to hear the rest. What happened next?"

Addie sat up and wiped her eyes carefully. "Blood splattered everywhere. He fell to the carpet. I screamed. Caz yelled. We both rushed to the man to see if he was still alive."

She steadied herself as she told the rest. "I called 911. Caz tore off his shirt and tried to stop the bleeding. He began compressions to make sure the man kept breathing. The stalker didn't say anything."

"Objection. Witness is characterizing a wounded man as a stalker without evidence." The D.A. was still trying.

Addie looked at the judge for his decision.

"I'll sustain that. Continue to call him the intruder."

"Yes, your honor. The intruder was silent," Addie said.

Marty continued. "Did you speak to him or did he speak to you?"

"After he shot himself, the intruder did not speak at all. Even after the EMTs arrived and worked to revive him. Even when they carried him out on a stretcher."

Marty turned to the judge.

"Your honor, I end my cross-examination."

The D.A. stood up. "I call as my next witness, Caz Cassidy."

Addie started to leave the witness box.

"Hold on a minute." The judge said. "The state and counsel will approach the bench." He instructed the bailiff to turn off the microphones.

They walked to stand in front of him. Addie stayed where she was.

"State, do you have forensic evidence indicating that the defendant used a gun that night?"

"No, your honor."

"Do you have any witness who claims that Leslie Tone did not shoot himself?"

"No, your honor."

"Do you expect the defendant to incriminate himself and admit to the shooting?"

"No, your honor."

"Counsel, what about you?"

"We've already heard the eyewitness testimony. Leslie Tone

shot himself."

"Then I don't see any point in wasting any more of the court's time. Stand down."

The D.A. and defense attorney returned to their places. Before Addie could make a move, the judge signaled to reopen his microphone.

"The court finds that no crime of assault with a deadly weapon was committed, and recommends that the District Attorney charge Leslie Tone with breaking and entering and criminal trespass. This case is dismissed. The defendant is released without prejudice." The judge banged his gavel.

Pandemonium broke out in the courtroom.

# Chapter 13

"Wow. That was a dramatic turn of events," Tess said. She and Miss Betty watched the crowds surge around the courtroom as the television announcer made excited comments about the case. Baron sat at the kitchen table, also watching.

"Too bad the judge insisted on turning off the microphones when he consulted with the lawyers," Tess said.

"Addie was right there. She must have heard what they said."

"Her testimony ended the trial before it began."

"No wonder she was so firm about needin' to get back to Jackson Hole," Miss Betty said.

"Without her, they would have put Caz Cassidy on the stand," Tess said.

"That nasty D.A. wanted to do it, too. You can see how red-faced he is. Humiliated," Miss Betty said, gesturing at the screen.

"What was the point of this trial?" Tess asked.

"Grandstanding," Baron said. "The D.A. wants to make a name for himself."

"So he tries to make up somethin' dirty between Addie and her friend. Shame on that District Attorney," Miss Betty said.

"Even if Addie was having a raging affair with Caz Cassidy, it's not a crime," Tess said.

Baron winced. "She said he was only her friend."

Miss Betty looked at him with pity. "Go on believin' that, boy, if it makes you feel better."

"She wouldn't lie under oath," he said.

"The girl left a lot out," Miss Betty said. "They been friends a long time. Coulda done some experimentin' even back when they was on TV together."

"Why Miss Betty, I'm surprised at you. I thought you believed Adrienne Jelleff walked on water." Tess put her arm around the older woman, and filched a bite of the chicken salad she was making. Miss Betty swatted her hand away from the bowl.

"Nope. She's human. I'm just sayin' she might have scratched an itch with that handsome boy a time or two in the past."

"I know I would." Tess laughed. "Caz Cassidy is gorgeous."

"You okay with that, boss?" Miss Betty asked. "Or are you still thinkin' that Addie is some kind of—?"

"Don't say it," he said. "Leave that sort of talk to the sleazy television commentators."

"That dirty-minded D.A. His mama should've washed his mouth out with soap a few times," Miss Betty said. "Would've done him some good."

Baron said, "Addie should have done that to me when I accused her of being a drug addict."

"She told you enough times she wasn't," Miss Betty said, pointing her wooden spoon at Baron.

"I didn't listen. Instead, I took it upon myself to be both judge and jury," he said.

"I hope you learned your lesson now, boy. That's no way to treat a woman."

"No," he agreed.

"Well, now the trial's over, I guess you'll be headin' to Jackson Hole to get on with your courtin'."

"What?"

"You aren't going to give up with Addie, are you?" Tess asked. "Besides, you owe her an apology." She smirked at him. "Better wear knee pads because you'll be doing a lot of crawling."

"Brat."

Miss Betty cackled. "That you will. Addie's just the woman to make you spell it all out." She slanted a sharp look at Baron as she set the bowl on the table.

"Hie yourself up to town, boy, before some other man decides to woo a talented horse trainer who's also a fine actress."

"You think she was acting today?"

"There goes your suspicious mind again," Tess said.

"'Course she was, boy. She had to save her friend, keep him off the stand."

"What secret was she hiding?" he asked.

"Why don't you take your dirty suspicious mind to Jackson Hole and ask Addie?" Tess said. "If she'll even talk to you."

"You're lucky she don't bring a lawsuit against you for

keepin' her here against her will." Miss Betty said, "Although she's not that kind."

"Yeah, she's way too good for you." Tess added, clearly enjoying piling on.

Baron finished his meal and stood. He grabbed his hat from the wall rack. "I've got some thinking to do."

The women nodded to each other.

***

In Jackson Hole, back at Caz's hotel suite, Addie asked Marty when the media circus would end. "I want to go back to my ranch and put it up for sale."

"You were impressive on the stand," Marty said. "Offers of new roles will pour in."

"Which I'll turn down without regret."

"Is the D.A. going to prosecute Tone for trespass?" Caz asked, ever anxious.

"Only if Addie presses charges."

She rolled her eyes. "Start up the frenzy all over again? No way. He can walk."

"He'll go back to following me around again," Caz complained. "I'll have to get a restraining order against him."

Marty nodded. "Already in the works." The lawyer continued, "We can also threaten him directly by suggesting that Addie will press charges. Unfortunately, nuts like that usually don't care."

Addie said, "You'll have a head start getting back to L.A., since he's still in the hospital."

"He'll sell his side of it to the tabloids," Caz fretted.

"If you ignore him and you're not involved in a trial, it won't matter," she said.

"No one will pay him any attention even if we have to go to court," Marty said. "It happens all the time in L.A. It might not even make the front page. Anyway, who reads newspapers anymore?"

Caz still didn't look appeased. Marty said, "Look, I know this isn't a happy ending. If he'd been a better shot, you'd never have to think about him again."

"Talk about callous." Addie shook her head. She stood. "Okay, guys, I'm done. Time for me to go home."

After thanks all around, and an emotion-filled embrace from Caz, she was ready to leave. "I'll let you know where I move to," she promised. "Don't come visit."

*** 

In the limo Marty had arranged, having avoided some but not all of the reporters after she left the safety of Caz's suite, Addie considered her next step. There still were dozens of reporters who wanted a piece of her, and once she was home, they'd be crawling all over her property. She'd have to deal. She couldn't have stayed cooped up in Caz's hotel suite a moment longer.

Had Baron seen her on TV? Had he guessed a little about why she'd had to testify? Or was he happy to be rid of her, and thinking only about running the ranch, or his abandoned geology career?

Had Tess and Paula gotten in trouble with Baron for flying

Addie out? She hoped not. They had saved the day. Would he ever have harmed her? Wasn't the chemistry mutual, with him feeling it as strongly as she did? He'd admitted to kissing her when he hadn't meant to. He'd been as physically compelled as she was. That was no excuse for not controlling himself, though, or acting domineering.

She had to get on with her life, yet she couldn't completely turn off thoughts about Baron. She wished he was here so they could talk it all out. Hoping he might want to see her again. Hoping it wasn't completely over.

The next move was up to him. Meanwhile, she intended to sell her ranch. On her way to her new home, wherever that might be, maybe she'd call him. It could be months from now. Or never. Did she even want to pursue a relationship with a man who had treated her so badly? He hadn't exactly abused her until the end, but initially he'd forced her to stay at the ranch, and he'd ordered her around repeatedly. He'd constantly tried to get her to make love with him, too, although trying to seduce her wasn't a crime, exactly.

Why was she thinking about Baron, when she could see a couple of cars full of tabloid reporters tailing the limo?

# Chapter 14

A week later, with the help of the local police, Addie finally was reporter-free. She hadn't seen one all morning. The trial was old news at last, at least on the national level. In Jackson Hole, it would reverberate for years to come. This was a small town except during ski season. She would not be able to avoid the whispers and stares. Even if she hadn't been at the center of a media frenzy, she'd now become an object of fascination because of her television background. It had only been a matter of time. She'd been living in a dream world about Jackson Hole being the right place to settle.

She'd made the call to her real estate agent. The ranch was already on the market. The smart thing would be to leave town immediately. She couldn't quite bring herself to vanish, though. Some part of her hoped to hear from Baron, or Paula, or Miss Betty, or even Tess. Why hadn't he tried to contact Addie?

As the number of tabloid reporters bothering her had declined, her thoughts had gone increasingly to Baron. The trial was over. Her need for secrecy was over. Was her relationship with Baron also over?

***

She'd just finished training Jefferson for the morning and had left the corral when a man appeared from the shadows of the stables. He was youngish, dressed in a casual jacket and khakis. Another reporter?

She did a double-take.

"Do you know who I am?" he asked.

"Leslie Tone," she replied, her mouth suddenly dry.

"The hospital declared me recovered. I checked myself out."

"Uh…that's nice," she said, edging toward the corral gate.

"I wanted to pay you a visit before I left for California." He moved between her and the corral.

She slightly switched directions. The tack room had a door that locked.

"Oh, no, you don't," he said, grabbing her arm in a powerful grip.

"Let me go." She struggled, but he was much stronger than her.

"I have something to say to you." His eyes held a crazed expression.

"Then talk. I'll listen."

He didn't let go of her arm, but twisted it instead. She gasped in pain.

"You took Caz from me."

"Caz and I are just friends."

"You lied. You didn't tell the D.A. that Caz and I were lovers." He twisted her arm harder.

She fought not to show the pain.

"You made it sound like I'm some kind of star-obsessed Hollywood fan." He twisted her arm again.

Involuntary tears dripped from her eyes. "Let go of me. I never did anything to you."

"You pretended Caz and I were nothing. You made me sound crazy," he screamed.

"Let me go." She twisted and struggled. Suddenly, his grip loosened, and she fell.

He drew a gun from inside his jacket and pointed it at her. "You'll pay for what you did."

She tried to stand, but he motioned with the gun to stay put. She raised her hands in a pleading gesture. "You don't want to do this. You'll go to prison."

"If I can't have Caz, neither can you."

She tried to shift a little, but he kept waving the gun at her.

Jefferson whinnied and raced toward them, although he was safely confined in his corral. Tone turned his head slightly at the noise. Suddenly, another horse flew at Tone, knocking him down.

"Whitey!" she cried.

Baron leapt from the stallion, which he'd ridden bareback. He quickly grabbed the man's gun and wrestled him face down on the ground. Baron planted his foot in Tone's back and put the gun to his head. "Easy does it. Don't give me an excuse to end your miserable life."

She scrambled up.

"Baron. How—?"

"Call 911."

"Right." She hauled her cell phone from her pocket and made the call. After she'd done it, she couldn't help giggling.

Baron shot her a curious glance.

"Convenient to have my phone," she said, arching an eyebrow.

Despite their tense situation, his face flushed.

***

Hours later, the police had come and gone. Addie had been examined by paramedics and her bruises photographed. Leslie Tone had been handcuffed, read his rights, and put in the back of a cruiser. The police had taken Addie's testimony and Baron's. She'd assured them she would press charges. Baron had volunteered to be her witness and had called a local lawyer and retained him to protect Addie's rights and urge the arraigning judge not to grant bail.

"I can't believe I have to go to court again," she said, as they watched the last police cars leave.

Baron said, "This time, the D.A. will be on your side."

She shook her head. "He hates my guts."

Baron frowned. "The Selkirks know a lot of people in this state. I'll make sure he gets the message to treat you with kid gloves."

Her mouth dropped open. "That easily? I should have met you sooner," she said. "You could have nipped Caz's troubles in the bud."

She had tucked Whitey in a paddock before the police arrived. Now she gave him some much needed patting and cooing in his new home. She soothed Jefferson, too. Baron stood beside her, watching, an odd expression on his face.

"That was quick thinking, to launch Whitey at him," Addie said.

"I had to trust that Tone wouldn't automatically shoot a horse."

"Good diversion."

"Whitey's yours now. A gift. Thought you'd like to have him."

"Thanks. He's a wonderful horse," she said.

Conversation dried up. She stopped petting the animal and faced Baron. They stared at each other. He looked tired and sad, yet was as handsome and impressive as ever. There were bandages on his hands.

"What happened to your hands?" she asked.

"The cabin burned down that night. I searched for you," he said, a look of remembered horror in his eyes.

"Oh, my god!" she cried on an indrawn breath.

"Served me right."

She flew into his arms. They kissed and touched and took inventory. "I shouldn't do this," she said, between the kisses she rained on his lips and his cheeks and wherever she could reach on his tall, solid body. "I should make you grovel," she said, punching at his chest. "You big bully," she said, kissing him with everything she had.

Despite the bandages, he picked her up in his arms as if she weighed nothing. "Where's your bedroom?"

Just as quickly, he set her down. Baron stepped back and stared at her. "What's wrong with this picture? Why aren't you fighting me?"

"It's simple." She put her hands on her hips. "I'm not your captive anymore."

\*\*\*

Baron lay on Addie's bed, one arm around her warm flesh, silently reviewing the last hour. To his shock, Addie hadn't fought him the way she'd always fought him before. Instead, she'd led him to her bedroom, enthusiastically shucked her clothes, and helped him do the same when his bandaged hands couldn't move fast enough. She'd pushed him down on her bed and climbed on top of him and kissed him silly.

The rest was even better, a haze of emotion and sensation such as he'd never experienced in his life. With her gentle hands roaming his body, she'd set about to relieve every ache his lustful thoughts had created during their standoff on the ranch. And more. Their lovemaking was beyond anything he'd fantasized. Addie was the woman for him, no question.

Did she feel as satisfied and happy at this moment? Did she share the incredible sense of peace and homecoming he felt because their arms were around each other and their bare skin was touching from shoulder to toe?

How could she possibly forgive him for what he'd done? He'd behaved like the lowest sort of animal. He didn't deserve a woman as fine as Addie.

He removed his arm from around her and sat up. Spying his clothes, he got off the bed and began to dress as quickly as he could.

Addie stretched and smiled languidly. "In a hurry, cowboy?"

"I shouldn't be here," he muttered. "How can you be so generous with a man who wronged you as badly as I have?"

Addie was silent as she donned her dainty underwear and covered it with her practical western garb.

"You should have made me crawl," he finally said as he buttoned his shirt over his chest.

\*\*\*

The words of a man who carried a load of guilt. Addie was too happy and too satisfied at this moment to want him to wallow in it. Every instinct about making love with Baron had been proved right. Strong, yet tender. Dominating, yet sensitive to her needs. He was the man for her.

Time to lighten him up a little. She cinched the belt of her jeans. "Who says I won't make you crawl?"

She raised an eyebrow. "I'm on my own territory now. I'm in charge." She continued, with a sly smile, "After days of ordering you around and restricting your freedom, maybe I'll lock you up someplace."

"Don't," he said. His expression was bleak. "For the longest hour of my life, I thought you'd burned to death."

She put her arms around him and hugged him with all her strength. He shuddered in her embrace. "I couldn't find you," he said in a low, hoarse voice. "I knew your death was on my hands."

"Your poor hands," she said, gently holding one bandaged paw. "You burned yourself."

"I had to find you." He drew the back of his other hand

across her cheek. The soft gauze caressed her skin. "I turned over every stick of wood, every piece of roof, everything."

"I was gone before the fire happened. I was never in danger."

"You were. I put you in that cabin. I had no right. I couldn't have lived with myself if you'd come to harm," he said.

"I didn't." She caressed his cheek. "I must have accidentally started the fire when I set some soup on to boil. It was one of my surprises in case you came back in a bad mood," she said, finding humor in it now.

"I'll bet." His mouth quirked a little.

"In the excitement of escaping, I forgot about the pot on the stove. I'm sorry I destroyed your property."

"Be serious." He broke away from their embrace and took an unhappy turn around the room. "That cabin was the scene of the worst behavior of my life. It's only right that it should be consumed by fire. I wish I could forget as easily."

"I should have told you flat out why I had to testify at Caz's trial. Revealed my past instead of hiding it," she said, all teasing gone.

"Then the memory of how Hollywood destroyed Julie would have come between us."

She nodded. "Which is exactly why I never told you." She led the way out of the bedroom, to the kitchen, where she pulled a coffee machine forward on a counter.

"You were amazing in court," he said.

"You watched?" She glanced back at him.

"You handled that D.A. so smoothly. I would have blown up at him."

She turned to look directly at Baron, bracing her hands behind her on the counter. "What are you going to do about your temper?"

He rubbed the back of his neck. "Stop pretending I'm cut out to be a leader of men. You got the worst of it, and I'm sorry."

"You kept trying to control me because the ranch hands didn't obey you?" Was it really that simple? Misplaced male dominance issues? "That can't have been the only reason."

"Julie, too." He paced around the kitchen restlessly. "You know how my thoughts went about your situation seeming to be like hers."

"Unfortunately, I do."

Baron said, "I'm going to learn how to control my anger."

"Go on." She cocked her head. "I'm listening."

"Things are going to change on the Selkirk ranch." He indicated the bandages on his hands. "As soon as these come off, I'm heading for Cheyenne to lay it on the line with my father."

"What will you tell him?"

"That the current setup isn't working."

"Then what? Will you leave the ranch?" she asked.

"I'll stay, if he returns. Remember that sandstone cliff? I want to develop it. Look for dinosaur bones. I'd still help on the ranch when needed, but I'd be a geologist again."

"What if your father refuses?"

"I'll hire a ranch manager and walk away. Return to geology elsewhere. I'm not cut out for running a ranch."

Just walk away? She doubted it would be so easy to relinquish his burden. In a standoff between two strong-willed men, the Selkirk patriarch and Baron, which would win? Could his younger brother ever recover enough to take over?

She pulled out two mugs from an upper cabinet. After she set them on the counter next to the coffee machine, her hands stilled. Who eventually ran the Selkirk ranch was not her concern. Baron was. She took a deep breath and faced him again. "What else do you plan to do about your anger problem?"

"I've signed up for anger management therapy. Already had my first two sessions." He prowled around the island, then sent her a wry look. "I want the old me back. I want to be a man you have no reason to fear."

"I'm not afraid of you," she said. "I never have been."

He expelled a breath. "I don't deserve your trust, but I'll work to earn it."

"What about Julie? If you see her ghost every time you look at me, we're still in trouble."

"You're different. There's no stardust in your eyes," he said.

Addie shrugged. "There's nothing so special about acting." She set the coffee brewing. "Let's check on Whitey."

As they walked to the paddock, she told him about her friendship with Caz, and about Caz's anxiety over his reputation. Baron showed no sign of jealousy or anger.

At the paddock, Whitey acted nervous. Addie called to him and began to coo in a low tone. The stallion responded instantly with a whinny. He raced to the paddock fence. Addie extended one arm and stroked White's neck under his mane, all the while making soothing noises.

"I'm envying the horse." Baron said.

She leveled an inquiring glance at him.

"I want you to coo at me that way, Addie," he said, open longing in his voice and on his face. "I want to feel that you care for me."

She stopped petting Whitey's neck. "We neither of us have said it, have we?"

"Said what?"

"I love you, that's what." She moved closer and put one palm on Baron's chest. "I do. I do love you, Baron. That's why it hurt so much when you acted like a crazy bully."

He gathered her into his arms. "I love you, too. I loved you from the moment I saw you stumble in the elevator. You were so beautiful."

"So sick."

"I wanted to protect you and take care of you," he said.

She gave him a disbelieving look.

"And make love to you then and there, but caring for my woman and protecting her is a large part of it. Yet I treated you badly and put you in danger. I regret that. I'll always regret that." His eyes showed his sadness.

"I forgive you," she said. "Now you must forgive yourself."

# Epilogue

Baron touched base with his ranch by phone, with Addie sitting close to him on the living room couch. After he was done, Addie welcomed the opportunity to chat with Miss Betty.

"Well, how you doin'?" came the older woman's voice. "That boy treatin' you right?"

Addie leaned back in Baron's loving arms, enjoying how one of his big hands caressed her shoulder. "Yes, he is, Miss Betty. He's treating me just fine."

"We miss you down here. Has he popped the question yet?"

Addie held her hand over the phone. "She wants to know if you've proposed yet," she told Baron.

"No, I haven't..." He leaned closer to speak into the phone, "and don't go spoiling any of my surprises, either."

When the joking call ended, Addie looked at Baron and asked, "What surprises, besides giving me Whitey?"

He gently disentangled her from his arms and rose. "You haven't made me crawl yet, so I'm starting on my own." He dropped to one knee in front of her and pulled out a ring box. He didn't open it, but placed it in her hands.

"Adrienne Jelleff, ex-actor, professional horse whisperer, captor of my heart, will you consider opening this box a year from now?"

Her breath caught. Her lips wanted to smile but her eyes were suddenly wet with tears.

"There's an engagement ring inside," he said, pressing her fingers around the blue velvet box.

When she said nothing, he added. "I won't ask you to take a chance on me today." He held her hands in his, so they clasped the ring box together. "It took me a year on the ranch to turn into an idiot. I figure it could take me another year to straighten up. After that, I'm hoping you and I have a future together. Will you think about it?"

His heart was in his eyes as he waited for her answer.

Finally, she nodded, as the tears leaked from her own eyes. "I will."

The End

FREE BOOK: Join my newsletter list and receive the free exclusive novella, *Carrie's Story*, which links to the Selkirk Family Ranch series and to *Cleaning Her House*. Go to irenevartanoff.com to sign up.

# A Note from the Author

Thank you for reading *Captive of the Cattle Baron*. If you enjoyed this book, please tell your friends, and consider reviewing it wherever you like to post reviews.

If you'd like to be notified when my next story comes out, please go to my website, irenevartanoff.com, to join my mailing list. I promise I'll keep your info private and only contact you when I am announcing a new story.

# Acknowledgments

In fine tuning and polishing this story I benefited from the valuable advice of numerous anonymous writing contest judges (*Captive of the Cattle Baron* has won awards in several writing contests), plus the reactions of several beta readers, including Kenya Brunson, Kathy Richardson, and Cris Warner. Author/editors Kathryn Johnson and Tom King devoted much time and effort to telling me in detail what ought to be fixed and what I could leave for readers to enjoy. I thank everyone for their help.

Irene Vartanoff

Made in the USA
Columbia, SC
02 November 2020